Prologue Of Seduction

Sexy Stories Collection

VOLUME 39

12 HISTORICAL EROTIC SHORT STORIES

KELLIE GRANIER

Publisher's Note: This is a work of fiction. Names, characters, places, and incidents are a product of the author's imagination. Locales and public names are sometimes used for atmospheric purposes. Any resemblance to actual people, living or dead, or to businesses, companies, events, institutions, or locales is completely coincidental.

Prologue of Seduction/ Kellie Granier. -- 1st ed.
Xplicit Press, an imprint of TLM Media LLC

ISBN-13: 978-1-62327-570-9
ISBN-10: 1-62327-570-9
eISBN: 978-1-62327-620-1

Printed in the United States of America

CONTENTS

1 CAROLINA INTERLUDE

It's 1862 and there seems to be no end to the fighting between the Yankees and the Confederates. Bret Butler knows there's no hope for the South, but he still admires the men fighting. One man in particular has always caught in his eye, and when he finds Ashley Wilkinson in a hospital in Charleston, he knows he can't let the opportunity pass him by. They're going to have at least one good night together in the middle of hell.

Vivien was a smart girl, but she could only work with the information given to her. Her mother and her mommy worked so hard to shield her from so many of life's truths that it wasn't a surprise there were holes in her knowledge, moments of such oblivious ignorance that Bret could only smile and try to stop himself from laughing at her sometimes. Her continuing, eternal fascination with Ashley Wilkinson was the most glaring example. She pined after him like a little girl, her eyes as big as saucers, her heart on her sleeve, and she was absolutely incapable of understanding that Ashley didn't love her that way—could never love her that way. There were all types of men in this world, and Ashley simply wasn't built to love a woman like Vivien. And the tragedy was that Vivien would never understand why, not even after Bret had tried to tell her. Even though Ashley's actual wife seemed to understand on some level, seemed to accept it—at least, she never behaved like Vivien, pushing the man to be something he wasn't, to take something he didn't want.

Bret had always had Ashley's number. He'd seen a lot of the world since he was cast out of public society—seen a lot and then experienced all of it. From the first meeting at Twelve Oaks, he realized the truth. He not only realized it, he felt the truth tug at him, felt it vibrate through him as it struck a chord deep inside. Bret was a man who knew what he wanted, society and rules be damned. He didn't change his mind once he made it up, and he knew his own tastes, his own desires, and the pleasure he hoped to sow, to reap.

He knew from the first meeting with Ashley that he wanted him, but he didn't resolve to act on that desire until after he met Vivien. The thought of taking the one thing the spoiled brat wanted but could never have delighted him. But due to the rather inconvenient War, his plans were delayed. Delayed but never forgotten.

Bret found Ashley convalescing in a hospital in North Carolina. Field hospitals were not exactly Bret's favorite places, but he tended to ask after a Captain Wilkinson when his various affairs and duties brought him to a new town, and he got lucky. He sent his boy around to the hospital with a few pieces of silver to give to the doctor in charge and directions for Ashley to join him.

"The ground is no place for a gentleman like yourself. Rest your bones in a bed tonight." Had been the words that had been written on the message.

Once upon a time, Ashley would have had too much southern integrity to ever accept Bret's invitation, but Bret knew that Ashley would come because he was a creature of certain comforts, and a lifetime of upbringing and training couldn't be forgotten even during the horrors of war.

The sharp rap on the door came a little

later than expected, but come it did. Bret opened the door for Captain Wilkinson, smiling broadly in the face of Ashley's suspicious and tired frown. He looked sickly—more yellow than usual—and his eyes were a dull gray, but he walked under his own power and he still moved with the inborn grace of a man of his breeding and status. It was too bad for him that the world he'd been bred and trained for no longer existed and would never come back. If Ashley survived this conflict, he'd be left to navigate in a land far beyond anything he ever imagined. Did he see that yet? Bret didn't know. Most things that were so self-evident to him seemed to be obscured to everybody else.

"Ash, Captain Wilkinson, it's so good to see you. Please, come in and have a seat. I just had supper brought up. I trust you're hungry." Bret smiled and ushered him inside.

Ashley still looked skeptical and wan, and he lowered himself stiffly into a chair while Bret busied himself with preparing two plates, filling them both with all the delectable delicacies he could find in Charleston. Not that there was much. It was clear to him that he was going to have to start running blockades if he wanted to survive this little conflict with a semblance of his sanity. Most people thought he was greedy, but it wasn't that he wanted everything. He just wanted his few comforts like any civilized person.

"I almost didn't come tonight."

"I'm not surprised. To what do I owe the pleasure of your company?"

"I was hoping you would have news of my family. I haven't received a letter in months, and I haven't been able to find the paper to pen my own. Please. If you could tell me..."

"Melanie is well."

"And everybody else?"

"Your Aunt Pitty is as silly as ever, and your sisters are both doing you proud volunteering. They're working as hard at home for you boys as they can."

His smile was relieved but a little strained. "And...everybody else?"

"If you want to ask me about Vivien, then be a man about it and speak up."

He looked down to his plate, and they both ate in silence, though Bret never took his eyes from Ashley. He studied every inch of him, noted every twitch and fidget, the stiffness in his movements, and the exhaustion around his mouth. He saw a man who was already bone-weary and still had decades of fighting and hard living ahead of him. After they finished up, Bret ordered his tub filled with hot water so Ashley could have a proper bath. Once submerged in the hot water with his belly full, Bret saw the tension drain from his face. He looked young again—much closer to his real age—and like the gentleman he was born to be.

"When you offered a bath, I didn't realize that you would be present."

"Why else would I offer you a bath?"

"I'm nothing but a bag of bones."

His ribs and hips did jut out more than normal, but not nearly as bad as they might have. Ashley's regiment still had enough food, though he had tucked away every single scrap Bret set in front of him, he was far from starved and it would be a few months yet before he looked truly emaciated.

"Perhaps, you can make yourself useful," Ashley suggested with a quirk of his brow.

Bret took the cigar from his mouth and left it smoking over a bowl on the side table. "You know me. Anything for our brave boys in gray." He removed his coat and unbuttoned his cuffs, rolling his sleeves up his elbows. His vest had already been discarded, and his suspenders hung down at his waist, forgotten. The only light came from a low-burning lamp in the corner. There was barely enough oil to last the night, and curfew was already in effect, but he left it burning, casting its warm golden light through the room. It even made Ashley look healthier; giving his skin the healthy golden shade it must had worn when his life was devoted to riding horses and other pursuits.

Bret knelt behind him and plunged his hands into the warm water. Fine-hand milled soap from France was another little luxury. It had been a mere trifle before, but by then, the ladies in Atlanta would pay anything for it. He worked up lather between his hands, bypassing the washrag in favor of his palms, wanting skin-on-skin contact. Bret craved it though technically that was one luxury the war hadn't interfered with and the blockade around the ports couldn't stop. There were just as many whores as before, and now, there were a new breed of widows and abandoned women who would gladly welcome a man into their lives for a night or a week or a month—however long he could stay. But they were a shallow comfort, and did nothing to satisfy the hunger in him.

Ashley's golden head dropped forward as Bret smoothed his hands over his shoulders, across his neck, up and down his back. He washed behind his ears and poured hot water over his head to wash his too-long curls. He scrubbed away the filth of the hospital and the battleground, searching for any injuries that may have been missed before. He invested himself into every detail, cleaning the dirt from beneath in his nails and in the wrinkly grooves of his knuckles. Ashley didn't fight him at all, didn't resist his attention or affection. There was nobody else like Ashley in the world—quite literally at the moment. He could only sell his affection to the whores, and he didn't even want them to have it. Vivien would sooner kill herself than extend one iota of warmth in his direction, much less accept the feelings he possessed for her. But Ashley wasn't like that. Ashley was enough of a gentleman to accept what Bret could offer, if only for a night.

His hands moved down Ashley's body, scrubbing over his hairless chest and his sunken belly. His prick was soft under the water, but Bret didn't let that discourage him from rubbing, washing, massaging, and squeezing until the flesh started to grow. He wiggled his fingers under his balls, testing the soft skin, touching him in a way that he was sure nobody else ever had. Bret couldn't imagine Ashley's proper little wife playing with his prick or giving his balls a nice little massage.

Ashley had been silent for most of the bath, but he couldn't stop his moans as Bret coaxed more blood to his groin.

"Captain Butler..."

"Don't you think we're past that now, Ashley?"

"We should not be doing this."

"Why not?"

"Because I'm a married man."

"It's war time."

"So?"

"So men do things they wouldn't normally do during war time. All of the rules have been suspended, and men can behave like animals once again. You wouldn't normally kill a man, would you?"

"No," Ashley admitted softly. "But that doesn't change the fact that I'm a married man."

"And you're breaking no promises to your lovely wife. She's a lady—my favorite lady—and I'd never do anything to hurt her. But I'm sure she would approve of me taking care of her beloved husband while he's so far from home. In fact, she'd probably be grateful for every kindness I extend."

"And that's what you think this is? A kindness?"

"What else would you call it? Would you like to go back to the hospital? I can't imagine you get much sleep there with the sounds of men dying surrounding you all night."

"What do you want from me?" Ashley asked, his voice low.

"I want you to dry yourself off and get

into the bed."

Ashley nodded and pushed himself to his feet, the dirty water cascading from his hair and shoulders. Bret wrapped him in a bath sheet, then turned down the bed, and stoked the fire while Ashley dried and prepared for bed. He didn't slip into the bed like a blushing bride on her wedding night, but rather, like the experienced and confident groom, and Bret found himself even more charmed by this strange man. He definitely didn't share Vivien's feelings for him, but he wished Vivien could see him as he did in that moment. She might see something she never expected.

Bret finished undressing and grabbed a phial of oil from his luggage before joining Ashley between the scratchy sheets. Scratchy or not, they were probably one of the few sets of sheets left in the entire city, and soon, they too would be sacrificed to the Glorious Cause, perhaps turned into bandages for the very man that Bret now reached for. Ashley didn't resist the embrace, fitting naturally against Bret's body as his arms went around him. For a moment, they did nothing but hold each other, their mouths a few inches apart, sharing warm breath.

"Captain Butler...Bret..."

"Do you want to be under me? Hmm? That's fine. I can give you what you want." He rolled Ashley onto his back, the little glass bottle still clutched in his hand. He settled on his knees and pushed Ashley's legs up and out, spreading them wide so he'd have access to his hole. He upended the bottle, coaxing the thick liquid from inside and rubbing it between his palms, spreading the slickness over his fingers. He stroked himself to hardness with one hand and rubbed Ashley's pucker with his other, working the oil over his opening before pushing his fingers deeper inside. He pumped his wrist, pushing deeper into Ashley's ass, moving slow and steady.

"Do you like this?" The question rumbled from Bret's chest.

Ashley nodded, but that wasn't good enough. Bret used more force to push his fingers inside and repeated himself. "Do you like this?"

"Y-yes. Yeeesss."

"Good. Because it's going to get better. I can promise you that."

Bret wasn't in any sort of hurry. They had the entire night, and he didn't want Ashley to experience a second of discomfort. He upended the bottle over his hand once more to ensure that Ashley's passage was slick, stretched, and ready. He had patience to spare, and so he carefully took Ashley apart, breaking him down inch by inch, until he was clutching the thin pillow over his face, blocking Bret's view of his gray eyes and the pleasure twisting his face. At first, Bret was the only one moving, but gradually Ashley lifted his hips and eventually pushed back. Bret purposefully slowed and slowed, until he was barely moving at all. Ashley moaned with frustration and pushed his ass forward, filling himself to the knuckle, then rocked back and did it again, harder than before. Bret added a third finger, twisting all three deep inside, as deep as he could, stroking his shaft as rapidly as Ashley rocked his hips.

Bret released his cock, spit in his palm, and then used the moisture to make the oil on his cock slick again. He scooted forward, positioning his cock at Ashley's entrance and yanking the pillow from his face. He needed to see him when it happened. And he wanted to be sure Ashley saw him, was looking at him and thinking about him and knew exactly who it was taking him. Ashley dropped his legs, locking them around Bret's waist and looked at him with heavy-lidded eyes. His earlier protests had been purely for the sake of appearances. His need was stamped on his face—and Bret could always see it clearly when somebody needed a good, hard fucking. That was Vivien's problem, too, but she didn't know it yet. She would one day, when they were both old enough to handle it, because Bret had no doubt that would be the day that changed everything for him, too.

With his cock wet and Ashley's ass slick and stretched, it was as easy as moving his hips. He slipped into the welcoming heat and sank deeper with a controlled thrust. Ashley's legs were locked around him and he pulled Bret deeper. Bret put both hands under Ashley's ass, lifting him to reposition the angle, then cradled him as he began to move, seeking the rhythm that would satisfy them both. But that wasn't all Bret wanted. He bent at the hips, claiming Ashley's mouth in a hard kiss. A kiss that was much too brutal for a lady's mouth, it was the sort of kiss that Vivien really needed to knock some sense into her head. He kissed Ashley as if it was all he wanted; as if Ashley was the only person he could ever want. It might have been unkind, but he knew Ashley wouldn't take it personally, wouldn't even let himself think about it again once he left the sanctuary of this hotel room. And even if Bret promised to care for him and protect him, he would leave and return to his regiment, take up arms even though he of all people understood the pointlessness of the whole damned endeavor.

But they kissed as if they were made for each other; like that small room was their entire world. Ashley clenched around him, squeezed him tight, and held him close.

Canons boomed in the distance, their thunder carrying for miles in the still night. The smell of gunpowder might have even tickled Bret's nose, though the sounds and smells of fighting were inescapable. The places that still enjoyed relative silence and peace were right on the edge of the precipice because things were going to get so much worse before they ever got better.

For some, things would never get better again. That was the reality Bret ignored as he lost himself in the simple, primal pleasure of Ashley's body. They moved together with precision, and Bret couldn't say for sure if it was Ashley's first time, but he sure didn't move like he didn't know what to expect. And Bret never saw a flash of pain on his face. Who had been the lucky man to claim him first? Bret was rarely envious as he rarely wanted something he couldn't have, but now, there were two streaks of envy running through him, he felt envy as green as Vivien's eyes. He wanted the love Vivien had for Ashley for himself. And he wanted Ashley for himself, as well. He hated, loathed, whoever had Ashley first.

"Harder," Ashley moaned.

Bret didn't immediately respond, so Ashley took control of the situation, like Bret hoped he would. He used his entire body to take over the rhythm, rising into each thrust with a forceful slam of his hips. The headboard beat an uneven tattoo against the wall, but that smoothed out, and soon, it was as steady and regular as any marching drum. A thud that seemed to echo the relentless pounding of his heart against his ribs and the jumping pulse at the base of his throat beat at his chest walls. When that rhythm, and his pulse, began to stutter again, he knew they were both close. Bret bore down, grinding his hips forward until Ashley's face registered something new. Bret timed it perfectly, reaching between them to fist his prick, stroking it rapidly until he felt the flesh jerk. His seed erupted from him, shooting long strings over Bret's stomach and chest while his body shook with the force of his climax. Bret quickly followed, his prick unable to withstand the sheer heat and pressure, the impossible pleasure in a world on fire.

2 THE COLD WAIT

The cold sank over the valley with the setting sun, settling over the erratic rows of tents, sinking into the bones of the shivering soldiers beneath the thin canvas. Ryan couldn't bring himself to leave the small, sputtering fire, though he knew the canvas might block the wind from slicing through him. All around him was the regular hustle and bustle of a busy camp, but the general chaos was relatively subdued. Everybody was too cold, too anxious, too tired, and there was no end to it. None that Ryan could see, none that any of them could see. They couldn't even count on death, since none of them knew when they'd ever engage with the Confederates again. It might be that night as the result of a surprise attack. It might not be until the spring, when the men (the ones who survived the starvation and disease of winter) finally thawed out and moved back into formation.

"Is this fire doing you any good?" Marsters asked as he squatted beside the tiny circle of heat. "You look like you're half-frozen."

"I am," Ryan said stiffly, finding it difficult to even move his mouth. His lips hurt, his fingers were numb, and he tried to wiggle his toes but he couldn't say for sure they were moving. "Everybody is. And it's just going to get worse."

"A-yup. But it might be better if you get out of the wind."

"No fire in the tent."

"There are other ways to stay warm," Marsters pointed out. "The fire is one way but not even the best way to chase away the chill."

"What are you talking about?"

"Come inside with me and I'll keep you warm."

Ryan swallowed, gazing at the hypnotic flames, holding his fingers out over the heat. He had once owned a pair of gloves but those were long gone, and there was nothing left to do except scrape together whatever rags he could to tie around his digits. So far, he'd done a fair job of protecting his skin against the weather, but the thin, torn rags wouldn't last forever.

"Did you hear me?"

"I heard you."

"Well?"

"There are too many people around."

"There are always people around. Besides, do you think we're the only ones? Come on, Ryan, open your eyes. We're bored, lonely, and freezing fucking cold. What else can we do?"

The simplicity of the argument was its greatest selling point. Not only were they bored, lonely, and cold, they were all sitting on the threshold of hell, patiently waiting for their number to be called. When the fighting started up again, most of them would be mowed down by canon fire and a rainstorm of bullets. Ryan had already watched his friends get killed. Now he didn't bother making friends, but Marsters didn't let that discourage him. Ryan didn't even remember how they first met, or why they were always together now. But it was definitely preferable to being alone.

He stood and ushered Marsters ahead of him, ducking into the tent and closing the flaps behind him. The canvas did shield them from the wind, but it did nothing to stop the cold from infiltrating even deeper. There wasn't even enough room to stand upright, but they managed to work around each other and dodge each other's elbows, stripping down to their underwear, heaping their clothes and both of their standard issue blankets over the top of their shivering frames. They smashed their bodies together, automatically seeking out the warmth of each other's bodies, moving without a single hint of shame. It was too cold, and the heat they could generate between them was far too promising to ignore. That was why Ryan ended up in Marsters' arms again and again, why he was willing to believe that "everybody" was doing this with somebody rather than acknowledge the truth that he was up to something he shouldn't be. He couldn't imagine the reaction if anybody ever found out, but that didn't stop him from pulling the buttons open so he could touch Marsters' hairy chest.

His fingers were like chunks of ice, but Marsters didn't pull away from the tentative touch. Instead, he covered the back of Ryan's hand and held his palm against his chest. He could feel the steady thump of his heart, and gradually he absorbed enough heat that the pain in his joints started to fade. He could move his fingers more freely, but the rest of him still felt like he'd spent too much time under a big block of ice. He slid his leg between Marsters' thighs, pushing himself closer. Marsters' fingers were freezing as they touched down, chilling him through the worn material of his underwear. But he couldn't pull away, as much as he wanted to. They were trying to warm each other, which meant the temporary discomfort of an icy touch would have to be endured.

They alternated, warming each body part in turn and peeling away the long underwear neither wanted to strip off themselves. Before long, they were completely naked, huddled together under the additional layer of their underwear, their skin-to-skin contact spreading the warmth and slowing the bouts of bitter shivering. The two men could not have been closer together, their bodies naturally fitting, pressed flushed from knee to neck. Marsters was hard, and just feeling his excitement was enough to bring Ryan's cock to life, too. It poked against Marsters' belly, undeniable evidence that this was about a little more than just getting warm. He hated that he could never hide his true reaction to Marsters. Especially since he used to have a modicum of control over the other man, but now that Marsters had seen the truth of the situation first-hand, there was no point in lying anymore. He wanted Marsters. He wanted him every day, every waking moment. He didn't know how to explain it because he had never felt anything remotely close to what he felt for Marsters for another man. But so many things had changed since the twice-damned war broke out that Ryan didn't know up from down, left from right.

They were happy to touch each other and steal small, silent kisses for a long time. There were still too many people awake to risk doing anything more, and though Marsters insisted that everybody was engaging in this sort of behavior, he didn't seem particularly willing to risk being found out. So while soldiers roamed through the camp, they would have to do everything in their power to be quiet. Later, if they were both up to it, they could go beyond the edge of the camp and do it properly, but it was so cold outside, and sneaking around the perimeter was fraught with its own peril, even if there weren't any enemies in the giant valley. Everybody's nerves were on a hair-trigger and ready to snap under the pressure of waiting. An unexpected rustle in the bushes could result in a hail of friendly fire that would not seem so friendly to those caught within it.

Ryan was smaller by a few inches and at least fifty pounds, and he wedged himself between Marsters' bulky frame and the ground, trying to create a cave of warmth for himself. Marsters had dark curly hair and a friendly face. It was impossible to say if he was twenty or forty--there was just something timeless about him. And there was something entrancing about his mouth. Something that made Ryan's core melt. He never knew any girls who could do so much to him with a simple touch and a sidelong look. Being so close to him, to his familiar scent and welcome heat, made Ryan hard, made him ache, and he honestly could not get close enough.

"I want to be inside of you," Marsters murmured, echoing his thoughts. His ass clenched and relaxed, his groin pulling tight, blood rushing from his head, but he still managed to murmured, "We can't right now."

"Why not?"

"Too many people around. Got to wait until they sleep at least."

"We'll be quiet. They'll never know it's happening."

Ryan moaned, ass clenching again. He wanted to. God, he really wanted to and maybe they could be quiet. Maybe they could get away with it, but what if somebody heard them? What if he opened his eyes to see their commander and the rest of the officers surrounding them, each looking down a barrel of a gun at the sodomites in their midst. Ryan didn't want to die, and a damned war was perilous enough without attracting hostility from their own side.

"I promise," Marsters whispered. "Nobody will hear. Nobody will ever know."

He pushed his hips down, grinding his prick against Ryan's thigh. His own prick grew another inch, hard and throbbing. It was hard to hear his own thoughts over the sound of his rushing blood, and he pulled Marsters down into a kiss to shut him up. He was too hard to deny Marsters again, so he tried to kiss the temptation away but that only made it worse. The nearest tent was only a few inches from Ryan's head, and the canvas separating them from their neighbors was so treacherously thin, as thin as the veil between life and death when the fighting started.

They didn't speak again, but they were still perfectly coordinated. Their bodies seemed to know what to do, and Ryan didn't consciously shift his hips, widen his legs, and slide more squarely beneath Marsters' trembling body. It was just more comfortable that way. It felt more natural. Their mouths moved together with simple familiarity, neither one of them doing anything particularly fancy. These kisses were meant to trap the moans, meant to offer more heat and more comfort, and if passion occasionally ignited between their mouths, that was a welcome bonus.

When Ryan felt Marsters' prick nudge his ass, he tried to move away. But there was nowhere to go except forward, and instead of breaking the contact between them, he pushed forward, taking the first inch past his tight pucker. He was dry, but he was still well-stretched and ready. Every day they walked closer and closer to that line, because every day he spread his legs like a two-bit whore and upped their chances of getting caught. Sometimes, he'd hide in his tent after lunch and use his fingers to stretch himself out, huddling under the blanket and working his thick digits in deeper and deeper. The more fingers he could fit, the better. He always berated himself for it, but he never regretted it. Especially when Marsters would slide right in like Ryan's ass was the perfect sheath and their bodies would meet with a slap, a sting, and a kiss.

Pleasure was the spark of heat that Ryan was missing. With his blood rushing faster and their bodies moving in silent rhythm, the cold, the death, the fear, all of it seemed much farther away. They swallowed down their moans and held their breaths, alternately kissing and slapping their palms over each other's mouths. Anything it took to keep down any suspicious noises. They were surrounded on all sides by dozens of men, and the din of the camp was constant enough to hide most things, only canon fire in the middle of camp would be able to obscure the shouts that Ryan wanted to shout. The pleasure was always intense, the closest thing to bliss that Ryan had ever known. It was a bliss he would have never known at home, where there was only one thing he could do, where his family expected him to get married and carry on the family name. And he would, if he survived this. But in the meantime, he wanted to get every second of happiness possible. He wanted to rise above everything because sooner or later, one way or the other, he'd be too far-gone to ever have another chance.

Marsters put his mouth next to Ryan's ear. "So close."

Ryan nodded his understanding. He slipped his hand between their tightly placed bodies and gripped his cock. His other hand went to the back of Marsters' head, and he forced their mouths together again. He stroked himself, bearing down on Marsters' cock as he rushed closer and closer to the edge, knowing that he was pulling Marsters along with him. If he timed it right, they would explode together, their bodies moving as one as they reached their shared goal. Their tongues fought and dueled, their teeth scraping over lips, and their bodies vibrating with moans they couldn't quite suppress. Marsters pounded down harder and harder, ramming his groin into the cushion of Ryan's ass. Ryan responded by stroking himself faster and then the line they were racing for was suddenly upon them. Ryan caught his breath as it felt like a hundred canons were shot at once beneath his skin and behind his eyes. He caught his own seed with his palm while Marsters shot himself deep in Ryan's ass.

They rocked together, their lips still fused, until they were both completely spent and soft. They came to a stop, but neither one of them made an effort to separate their bodies. Neither would ever risk losing the heat they'd just generated, especially with the fine sheen of sweat on their chests and the back of their necks. Ryan closed his eyes, willing himself to sleep so he could dream about someplace warm, somewhere happy.

3 A RETURN FROM PHILADELPHIA

It was a ten-day journey from Philadelphia, where the Continental Congress was held, and Nora felt every single one of those days keenly. She continued her daily routine without interruption, but her heart beat a little bit faster, and her feet seemed to move a little slower. Her loneliness, always so overwhelming, grew by the day, sharpened by the knowledge that soon it would be over. It might have been easier for her when her husband Josiah went to the Congressional Congress if she had a wee babe to care for, but though they tried very hard before he was elected to the seat in Congress, she never took with child. But he was coming home for the Christmas recess--a full two weeks--and if the weather cooperated and the roads remained clear, they could make the most out of all fourteen days.

She still received letters daily from him as she waited. The day she didn't receive a letter, her stomach erupted in a cloud of butterflies and she might have giggled and done a little dance. That meant he'd be home soon. He always arrived within a day or two of his last letter. She couldn't sit still for the rest of the day, and all of her darning, knitting, and writing would have to wait for a time when she could focus. She spent the day outside, tending to the animals and clearing snow from the yard, full of energy that she couldn't burn up. That night she barely slept at all and the next morning she jumped out of bed with the same anxious excitement, jumpy and jittery. Her aunt paid her a visit, forcing her to remain indoors for the vast majority of the day. A fact that Nora resented somewhat--until she had reason to be grateful that she didn't wear herself out shoveling snow.

Nora sent her aunt on her way home after supper and began her nightly ritual of securing and locking the house. She thought she heard horses outside, but she wasn't sure until she heard a sharp tap-tap-tap on the door. Her hand flew to her mouth with her sudden surge of excitement, and she crossed to the door, eager to lift the latch and throw it wide open. She didn't fear strangers on the other side of the lock. She knew the sound of her husband's knock. She opened the door to his wide, dear smile, and she barely squeaked out a "Jed" before throwing herself into his arms. He caught her with a laugh, twirling her around and holding her close to his broad chest. She tilted her chin, angling for a kiss but he surprised her by pulling back slightly.

"Nora, do you remember my friend Mr. Thomas Bartlett?"

Nora stepped back from her husband as the man stepped forward, suddenly shy. Not because she didn't know Mr. Bartlett, but because she knew him all too well. He'd once courted her, as her husband well knew. Thomas had even wanted to press for her hand, but she'd been distant with him, playing it cool, keeping him hanging on a string, until she knew for sure what Jed's feelings were. He stepped forward and bent to kiss her cheek.

"Hello, Nora. It's wonderful to see you again." The sound of his voice sent chills down her spine. Thomas was taller than average and extremely striking with an aristocratic face, piercing blue eyes, and a wild shock of black hair. He'd been the most attractive bachelor in the county, and unless she was completely behind on all the gossip, he was still the most attractive bachelor in the county. "And I apologize for my unannounced visit."

"It's my fault," Jed said, his arm going around her waist. She tilted her chin again and this time he did grace with a small kiss on the corner of her mouth. "I hope you don't mind dear, but I ran into him on the road and once we got to talking, I remembered how much we always had in common." He gave her a little squeeze and smiled down at her, and she returned the smile.

"Of course I don't mind. We have plenty of room for a guest. Now both of you get inside before we all freeze to death."

She ushered them inside and helped with their hats and heavy coats, getting them settled in front of the fire with a hot cup of tea for both of them. They were both ravenous from their journey and she was so happy to have her husband home that she didn't care about the late hour. She happily prepared them a large meal, listening as they regaled her with stories from their travels. It hadn't been an easy journey, especially with the number of surprise snow flurries they met on the road, but they both agreed it was worth it. Everything seemed completely normal through supper, right up until after Nora cleared the dishes away and it was time to retire to bed.

"Nora, come here, darling." Jed took her

by the hand and pulled her into his lap, wrapping his arms around her small frame. She looked at him expectantly, but he didn't say anything. He pulled at the pins keeping her hair secure until the braids unwound themselves from her head. He pulled the rest of the pins out and combed his fingers through her tresses until the braids were unbraided and her golden hair hung in soft waves down her shoulders. She wasn't surprised that he wanted her hair to be free--he always said it was his favorite part of her-- but she was stunned that he performed such an intimate act in front of Thomas. Why not wait until they retired to their bedroom? Thomas was watching. In fact, he seemed rather transfixed.

He gathered up her hair and pulled it over her left shoulder, exposing the right side of her neck. His other hand went to the buttons on the back of her dress, and she opened her mouth to protest but Jed's lips were suddenly pressed to hers, silencing her. She automatically tried to jerk away from the kiss, but the hand holding her hair wasn't letting her go anywhere, and she had no choice but to relax into the caress, her body welcoming the attention even as her mind raced with a million questions. It'd been so long since she'd touched her husband, since she felt his sweet lips and his probing tongue, and the reassuring solidity of his strong chest and thighs. Thomas's presence confused her, but nothing could distract her from the object of her nightly yearning.

While his mouth distracted her, his other hand continued to work on her buttons. He was good at it, popping each button free with his thumb and forefinger all the way from her neck to her waist. When she felt the material sliding away from her arms, she jerked away, blushing as she realized that Thomas could now see all of her under things.

"Husband, we should retire to our own room."

"I'm comfortable here."

"But...Thomas..."

He cupped her cheek, looking into her eyes. "Do you trust me, dear?"

"Of course I do."

"You know that I love you and I only want to do the best for you?"

"Yes. I would never think anything less."

"And do you like it when I touch you like this?" He ran his fingers down the back of her neck, ghosting the tips over her spine. She arched like a cat and shivered.

"Yes, Husband, you know I do."

"Do you think you might like it if, instead of only two hands, you felt four? And instead of one mouth worshipping your milky skin, there would be two?"

Her face flushed such a deep red that she thought her cheeks might well be on fire. Her eyes even tingled, as though irritated by smoke. "You want me to allow somebody other than you...other than my husband...to touch me? I don't understand. Why would you want that?"

"You don't have to do anything you don't want to do, darling. But I only want to give you as much pleasure as possible. And Thomas has always been a dear friend of mine. Yes, even when we were both wooing you and trying to win your hand. I'm thankful every day you chose me, but if you had selected him, I would have been content knowing that you'd be well loved and well cared for. That is to say, I trust him completely. And you, my lovely wife, I trust with my life."

"But you're my husband and I'm only meant to want to be with you."

"I'm your husband and I want you to have everything you want and more, everything you deserve. And he wants so much to touch you. Will you allow him that small privilege?"

Nora didn't know what to say, didn't know what to even think. She would never admit it out loud, but the only man she ever thought about besides her husband was Thomas. He'd haunted her dreams, and she'd been tempted to give into his love making more than once. But she always resisted because it was the right thing to do, because desiring him (more than loving him) was wrong and she was wrong to feel that way. If her husband was anybody else, she would suspect the laying of a trap, but he had no reason to doubt her fidelity or try to trap her. With that in mind, she gave a small incline of her head, signaling that Thomas could have that small privilege.

She didn't know exactly what to expect. She didn't know how he wanted to touch her or what he would do once his skin came in contact with hers. She didn't know how she'd react, or what Jed would do. She wasn't quite expecting the soft scrape of knuckles across her jaw or the oh-so-gentle caress of his thumb down her windpipe to her pulse. She swallowed, and his thumb lifted slightly. She knew her pulse was racing and he could feel it. She kept her gaze averted because she didn't want to reveal herself, especially since she had no idea what she was in danger of revealing. Jed tugged at the ties holding her corset closed, slowly loosening it while Thomas continued to caress her skin, moving over her collarbone and then lower, to the swell of her breast.

Nora caught her breath as he touched her, but Jed's mouth instantly went to the spot where her shoulder met her neck, and the gentle kiss first soothed her, and then became more distracting as he applied more pressure and let her feel the tips of his teeth. The faint hints of pain gave her a thrill, and goose bumps erupted across her skin from her throat to her tummy. Her nipples hardened in the process, forming into little rosy pebbles before Thomas even had the chance to touch her. But then the pad of his finger skimmed over her taut skin, straightening her spine and pulling a little moan from her throat. Jed's mouth moved into a smile and though she didn't understand it, she realized that he genuinely did find pleasure in allowing Thomas to touch her. She found the situation strange, there was no way around that, but she felt much more comfortable. As much as her pleasure concerned him, she wanted her husband to be happy. That was where she found her greatest happiness.

The two men made short work of the rest of her clothes, pulling her to her feet to finish removing everything that stood in their way. Once she was nude, blushing, and shivering, Jed swept her up in his arms and carried her into the bedroom, Thomas following directly on his heels. As he lowered her to the bed, Thomas lit the lamp on the bedside table, casting the room in a warm glow and allowing her to see both sets of eyes trained on her completely vulnerable body. She didn't know it was possible to blush everywhere, but she could feel a flush from her toes to her scalp. Or maybe that was merely the pressure of their combined gazes--their eyes seemed to be burning, searing a hole straight through her body.

Jed moved first, taking her arms and straightening them, then pulling each leg out, making her form an X on the bed. She wanted to cover herself, but Jed caught her wrists and gently pulled them away from her chest. He bent his head over one breast and Thomas did the same on the other side, their mouths going for her nipples, closing around the flesh at the same time. Thomas's hair was as dark as coal and Jed's was the color of freshly harvested honey. She lifted her now free hands and combed her fingers through both full heads of hair, marveling at how soft they both were. She half expected something to happen to her when she touched Thomas--perhaps a bolt of lightning from the heavens to disrupt her exploration, but nothing happened at all. Except Jed moaned softly and Thomas inhaled sharply and she shifted her attention, tracing the C-curves of their ears, and then moving along their square jaws.

Their lips were as gentle as a spring rain on her breasts, skimming over the fleshy globes but always returning to the perky peaks of her nipples. At first, she could keep her reaction under wraps, but the more they flickered their tongues over her skin, the harder it was to stay silent. Finally, she had no choice but to give in, the sharp sting of Thomas's fang over the tip of her tender flesh too much to withstand. It started as a moan, but then Thomas bit down and it turned into a whimper--a sound with a pleading edge to it. It felt so good, and she immediately wanted more. It wasn't like anything she ever felt before, and she couldn't quite put her finger on why. Maybe it was just as simple as two mouths creating twice as much heat, twice as much pleasure. Or maybe Thomas touched her like she never felt before. All she knew was that the heat was moving south, settling between her legs, and her flesh was starting to throb.

Thomas remained transfixed over her breasts but Jed started to move, kissing down her body. She had the sense that he was reacquainting himself with her entire body, greeting every part of her with his mouth after such a long absence. When he settled between her legs, she didn't know what to expect. All she knew was that she was tender, almost sore, in the most secret parts of her body. She was naked and sprawled, and every touch was ten times--a hundred times--more intense than she would have expected. Something deep inside tingled and clenched and she automatically rocked her hips, grinding her flesh against Jed's mouth. He flicked his tongue over her nub even faster, and she had to push his head away, panting for breath.

"I'm sorry, darling."

"No, it felt very good but it hurt, too."

"I know, that's why I apologized. You must be quite sensitive. I need to be mindful of that. How does this feel?"

He used his fingertip, applying slightly more pressure, pressing until she whimpered and wiggled her hips again. Thomas was still busy with her breasts, and the combined sensations lit a fire in her stomach. The heat spread through her limbs and settled at the base of her spine, the sweet pleasure rolling through her, cresting and then dipping with the motion of Jed's fingers. He was the moon controlling the tides through her body with a single touch, the swell of each wave taking her closer and closer to that final outcropping, where nothing existed except the sea of pleasure on all sides.

"Better," she breathed.

"Better? Good. Do you like it?"

"Yes." Still a high-pitched whisper of sound.

"Do you want more?"

Normally she would nod her head and ask for whatever she thought he wanted, but something about their new situation emboldened her. Clearly, they weren't playing by the same rules she'd been laboring under, and maybe if he could introduce something this unorthodox, she could try something, too?

"I want you."

"You have me, darling."

"No...no, I want you inside. Please, Jed, dear, I've been without you for so long. I miss you so much. I need you." She was saying it at the ceiling, and somehow not looking at him made it easier. But then he was suddenly filling her vision, looming over her while Thomas finally relented on his oral assault.

"It sounds like you'd better give her what she wants," Thomas said with a fond smile.

"Yes, I better had. Will you assist me?"

Nora's eyes widened, but then she realized that he only meant for Thomas to help him undress. She pushed herself up on her elbows, watching with shameless fascination as Thomas helped her husband remove his clothing, bit by bit, revealing his beautiful form. Thomas was attractive, but there was something poetic about her Jed. She tingled at the sight of him, her body flushing with new heat, and she felt a fresh slickness between her thighs. She was ready for him, ready to be taken and loved by him.

She expected Thomas to join them on the bed again, but he lingered as Jed took his place over her. She took him by the arms, moved her hands up to his shoulders and back, smoothing her palms over his unbroken, nearly flawless skin. The few scars she had found on him were old, the results of childish games. A draft moved through the room, making her shiver and her wet, taut nipples ached like fresh bruises. Her fingers automatically went to the twin sources of pain, but rubbing the pebbles did nothing to alleviate the problem. Thomas didn't miss the gesture, and he was at her side again within seconds. She wasn't sure what to say, and then he closed his hot, silky lips around her flesh and something about the act released the pain, letting it shoot through her body to pierce her nubbin. She felt it jerk, felt everything throbbing, and she lifted her hips to meet her husband's first downward thrust.

The first thrust was like sunshine piercing a deep fog, sending it scattering and heating everything. Her hand went to the back of Thomas's head, and she held him in place, fingers working through his hair while her palm guided the motions of his mouth, the flicks of his tongue. Jed hiked her legs up, bringing them over his shoulders and putting her feet straight in the air. The position made her feel awkward, but the angle was absolutely unbelievable, and more pleasure flooded through her.

Jed started to move his hips, pumping them against her and grinding down, but never taking his plug from her. He remained fully sheathed, filling her and stretching her and making her feel every inch of him. She held him with her left hand, her fingers gripping the bulging muscles in his upper arm while she clenched down, pushing her hips forward to meet his, grinding hard on his length. She never would have done that before, but something about the way Thomas touched her completely transformed her. Her body felt like it was brand new, like it belonged to somebody else. She couldn't understand the sensations or her reactions; all she knew was that she wanted more. She started to think about where else Thomas could kiss or touch her, the sensitive spots that lined her body from head to toe.

"Oh...oh darling...oh my sweet Nora...you feel so good. I'm sorry, I can't...I'm so close..."

She understood that he meant it would be over soon, that he was close to being soft again, but she didn't want this to be over. She felt like she was just getting started, and she knew that she'd not only be unsatisfied, but she'd be constantly aware of the empty place between her legs. It would keep her awake and burning with longing.

"Can...Can Mr. Bartlett...Can he...?"

"Can he what?" Thomas asked with an amused smile. It was hard to answer, hard to do anything with Jed rocking his hips with a faster, harder tempo.

"I'm not ready to stop," Nora admitted shyly.

"If that's what you want," Jed said, dropping her legs to wrap around his waist as he leaned over her. She welcomed the change in position, wrapping around him and lifting her head to meet his kiss. His tongue plunged into her mouth as he took one final thrust and she felt him shooting his seed deep into her womb. She moaned, tightened her legs and lifted her hips, taking every centimeter of him that she could. He rocked for a few more seconds, and then gently broke the kiss, gradually extracting himself from her. He moved from between her legs, allowing Thomas the room he needed to take his place.

But as soon as she saw a man who wasn't her husband settle between her legs, nerves gripped her and she forgot all about her carnal appetites. She wasn't sure if she was ready for this, but she wasn't sure if she should say anything. Thomas must have seen something on her face because he paused, "Are you scared?"

"I'm...I don't know. Yes. I'm not sure. I'm nervous."

Thomas looked up and met Jed's eyes. Some silent communication passed between them, and Thomas suddenly shifted direction and intention. She didn't know what he was doing until he had his mouth hovering over her mound. He held her lips open and dipped his head, letting his tongue glide over her nub. The pleasure was instantaneous, like slamming into a wall with great force. Every nerve woke, every muscle clenched, and every second slowed to an eternity as her body adjusted and responded to the sudden silky hot tongue sliding over her most sensitive parts.

She felt like she could climb out of her own skin. She clawed at Thomas, moaning and rocking, urging him to lick her faster, forgetting that the extreme sensation had been painful only minutes before. But now she was too close to the edge to care about pain because it just didn't hurt anymore. She felt a nudge at her opening and then two fingers were sinking into her slick channel. His fingers weren't as long or thick as her husband's member, of course, but she was like one giant, pulsing nerve. All he had to do was touch her inside and lick her outside, and she was breaking apart. She bucked wildly against his face, eyes closing and face twisting as the bliss pushed her to the highest point of pleasure. And there she stayed for what felt like an eternity. When she drifted down from that peak, Jed was there to catch her in his arms, and Thomas's hands were like gentle promises moving over her as she kept drifting, lower and lower, into a satisfying sleep. She felt fingers pulling apart the lips between her thighs and then a soft tunnel of air blew over her skin. She jerked with surprise, feeling as though he'd actually touched her. He put a steadying hand on her thigh and did it again, pursing his lips and blowing the air directly on her nub of singing nerves. Thomas kept his mouth on her nipple and reached across to her now abandoned breast, his fingers gently rubbing and pinching her nipple into strict attention. Sometimes he moved up to her throat, and sometimes he moved down to her stomach, but he stayed in the general range of her torso, leaving her lips--upper and lower--to her husband's attention.

4 THE HITTITIE SPY

The Hittite spy was brought to Prince Pareherwenemef as soon as he was caught in the Egyptian camp (though after he was given a beating that made his ears ring). He was thrown to the ground at Re's throne and kicked to his ribs to keep him down.

"We believe he has an accomplice, Sire."

"Has he spoken?" Re asked, eyes locked on the young man at his feet.

"No. But he's not recognized by any of the generals and there's no record of him."

"Leave us." He made a gesture that sent away all except his guards and his slaves. The Hittite remained in his kneeling position, head bowed and body trembling like a leaf. He was filthy and sun-chapped, and narrow and skinny though clearly not starving. He had a bruised cheek and a good sense to keep his eyes averted while Re studied him.

"What is your name?" When a response was not immediately forthcoming, Re barked the question again, this time with a blade in his hand.

"T-Telipinu," the man stuttered out.

"So you are a Hittite?"

He nodded miserably.

"That is too bad for you. We've lost many men in this war, and I'm sure the survivors would savor the opportunity for revenge. You should have tried harder not to get caught. But don't worry. I'm not going to turn you over to them. Not until I am finished with you."

"Please, Sire, I'll tell you anything you want to know. Just please, spare me."

"Spare you? The spy of my father's greatest enemy? You know that is not possible."

Telipinu looked up with imploring brown eyes, and Re was startled to realize that the spy was as beautiful as a woman, with smooth cheeks and full lips. What sort of people were the Hittites that they would send such a rare beauty into the heart of the enemy's camp? "Please, Sire. I will tell you anything, I will do anything, but please spare me. I was forced to come here, and since you have caught me, I'll carry no information away with me."

"You want me to spare you, but have you remained a prisoner?"

"Prisoner, slave, whatever you desire, as long as you don't kill me."

"I have no desire in killing sniveling women," Re spat. Maybe this boy really was a woman. "Stand up. Remove your coverings."

Telipinu immediately jumped to his feet and pulled his garments away, revealing a flat chest, narrow hips, and a small staff. Without his layers of garments, he looked even smaller, like Re could pick him up and snap him over his thigh. But he definitely wasn't a woman.

"What good are you to me alive? Your death will satisfy the gods and will send a clear message to your Hittite commanders that we will not tolerate spies. Get on your knees." Re adjusted his grip on his long dagger and rose. "Put your hands behind your back."

"Wait. Don't you want to know what I know about the Hittites?"

"What could a child like you possibly know?"

"I know many things, Sire. I was handpicked by King Muwatali himself from his personal harem. I have heard many things...and I've learned many things."

Re frowned. The boy was clearly desperate and could be making things up.

If he were lying, killing him would be much sweeter for the personal effect it would likely have on his father's rival. But then again, if he were telling the truth, then he could possess a great deal of intelligence necessary for strategy—information that could turn this battle into a victory rather than the desperate, grappling standstill they were currently engaged in. They hadn't expected Muwatali's charioteers to be so numerous or so skilled, and though Re's father led four regiments, only two were present and only one of those was still in condition to fight. The stakes were high here, but he had to be sure that the boy was going to give him actionable information.

"Prove it."

"Sire?"

"Prove you're who you say you are. Show me what you do in Muwatali's personal harem."

This was about more than the youth's willingness to do as requested; Re also planned to gauge his skill. If he fumbled, hesitated, or otherwise seemed unsure, Re would slash his throat in an instant and have his head on a stick for the Hittite forces to view. He had no doubt that they'd recognize a face that was once this pretty. The boy clearly wasn't stupid. Understanding passed through his wide eyes, and he dropped to his hands and knees to crawl to Re's lap.

Re kept his blade poised, waiting for one false move, as Telipinu fumbled with his robes, pushing them away from his soft staff. He gripped the base and immediately bent his head, bringing the flesh directly to his lips. He sucked gently on the crown, tongue wiggling like a slippery fist over his slit. Gradually, the spirit of arousal filled him and his staff began to harden in the boy's mouth. Soon he was at full stiffness, his member jutting forward, eagerly seeking more heat. Telipinu sank lower and lower, taking his mouth all the way to the base and letting Re's shaft slide down his throat without hesitation. He swallowed around the flesh, which was now throbbing and full to the point of leaking. He cupped Re's balls and tickled the tender skin behind the low-hanging bag while he swallowed.

Re had not been with a woman at all since they left Pi-Rameses to begin the campaign, but he still didn't expect to be quite so sensitive and willing. Heat climbed up his spine, marching resolutely up to his head while everything else seemed to be flowing in the direction of his groin. His heart felt like it was beating too rapidly. It almost felt like the moments before the order to fight were given but sweeter because it felt so amazing. Telipinu's throat was tight and hot, and it flexed around Re's shaft with so much pressure that he didn't know if he could take it. Weapons never took him down and he was stronger than any man in the regiment. As the son of Rameses II, he was an untouchable prince. But perhaps the key to his entire being was held in this captivating, enthusiastic youth.

He eased up and brought his lips back to Re's ridged crown. He sucked on it again but this time the sensations were much more intense. His free hand went to the armrest and he gripped it with white-knuckle intensity, using all of his strength to keep from doing anything as undignified as crying out. He couldn't moan his pleasure and he couldn't speak to demand the torture to stop. If he did either one of those things, then the boy would know that the prince was beaten. Re had never been beaten before, and he was not going to fall victim to his own test.

He sank back down, the heat enveloping him once again. His mouth was so wet; it made Re think of a sleepy oasis, a place to rest and replenish. Telipinu swallowed again, but now he was far more sensitive, and the sudden soft grip around his throbbing crown nearly pulled the dreaded moan from him. He forced it down, struggling to keep his face from giving everything away. He was losing control, and he didn't like it. He set the blade aside and reached for the boy's head, clasping it between his large palms. His head looked like a piece of fruit between his big hands, and all he had to do was twist. It would be a merciful kill since Telipinu would be dead before he even realized what was happening—much kinder than the blade.

But if he did that, the pleasure would end, and Re wasn't ready for that. He curled his fingers in the long, curly hair and flexed his grip, pulling tight and forcing Telipinu to look up with a shocked gasp. Re didn't give him time to form his question, yanking his head back down to his shaft and slamming his hips forward at the same time. The boy choked and gagged, but Re was already moving, pulling Telipinu up and off his staff and then slamming him down again. This time, the boy seemed better prepared and there was no gagging. By the third time, he seemed to understand what was going on and he relaxed, letting Re move him as if he was nothing more than a child's toy. There was no resistance in him as his throat fluttered and flexed, but there were soft moans as Re rammed into him with bruising strength.

He was surprised to realize that he found this far more pleasurable than he expected. He had concubines for this act, but none of them made such willing partners, and though he was setting and controlling the tempo, Telipinu was still doing a great deal of work with his mouth and his throat, his tongue sliding up and down the shaft. Even the occasional scrape and sting of his small, sharp teeth felt like it was calculated to earn a certain response and employed more often once Telipinu knew for sure that it worked. And it did work. Very, very well. Re loved the sudden red flash of pain bursting like the sun over the Nile and then fading into more golden pleasure that swirled and rolled through him.

He prided himself on his control. He had full rein over his passions and his emotions, such as they were. But sometimes, when he was fighting, some madness overwhelmed him and he fought like a possessed warrior. His men followed him into battle because they knew he would always be with them, fighting at their sides and defending their lives, but for him, it wasn't bravery. It was just a red haze of anger that fed on the blood and stench of war. He felt like that now—only it wasn't a blood lust. He fucked Telipinu's face harder, slamming him down with no other thought than the pursuit of his ultimate satisfaction.

When he felt the familiar tingle at the

base of his spine, he debated on pulling away and freeing his staff from the boy's throat. He was lower than the lowest in Re's kingdom and he didn't deserve the hot flood of Re's royal seed, but it felt too good to stop. He was greedy, waiting to accumulate every possible second of pleasure that he could possibly get. Who knew when he'd ever meet another who could open his throat and swallow like a serpent? He lifted himself from his throne, angling his hips to get his shaft as deep as possible. Telipinu gave his balls a gentle squeeze and tugged them like he was going to pull them right off. Re's first instinct was to knock him away, but as he was curling his hand into a fist, the pain suddenly transformed, just like the scrape of his teeth translating into something pleasurable.

"Oh. Oh." Two short sounds that were hardly anything at all but betrayed everything as he slammed forward one final time, his release rocking him down to his center. His hips moved without his control, jerking back and forth until he was finally empty and spent. Telipinu smiled down every drop of his seed, not letting a single bit slip from between his lips.

"Do you see, Sire?" Telipinu asked hopefully.

"Where is Muwatali now?"

Telipinu promptly named a location that was much, much closer than Re expected. Surprised, he asked again. And a third time. But Telipinu was insistent, and their meeting came to a prompt end as Re realized they were at much more risk than he had ever assumed. He ordered the royal family to break camp and prepare to flee to the west, instructing his generals to prepare for an attack. Telipinu watched the ensuing controlled chaos with fearful eyes, as though watching his own death.

"You'll remain as part of my household until after the battle," Re declared, his staff twitching as if in approval of the decision. He definitely wasn't done with this boy. He needed to know what other tricks he had learned in his service to the Hittite king. And then he intended to have Telipinu teach his concubines everything he knew.

5 THE GOOD YEAR RITUAL

The Sumerian King arrived to the Temple of Eanna as a king but entered it as a single man in simple robes, humbling himself to the goddess Ianna during her festival. No king ever protested, and there was never any thought of not satisfying the fickle goddess, as she could not only turn the crops bad but bring discord, chaos, and war down on the kingdom. The king brought offerings to burn on her alter--the finest calf, goat, and sheep from each flock--and the finest jewels to adorn her priestesses. He entered the Temple alone and performed the rites on his own while the High Priestess looked on with a watchful eye, noting every step of the rituals and making sure each rite was performed in full. When the king completed his tasks, she stepped forward and offered her hand.

"My Lord, Dumuzid, I am pleased you have returned to me."

He took her hand and bowed deeply, his mouth leaving reverent kisses on her knuckles. She led him to the bed behind the alter, carefully made up with the richest silks and turned to undress him. Even that part was deeply ritualized, and she took care to do it properly, respectfully shedding the garments to expose his mortal body. This king was still young, still a warrior only recently ascended to the throne, and his body was still hardened by war's unforgiving edge. He carried many scars and battle wounds, each one declaring his right to rule. He would have been a fine proxy for the Goddess's consort regardless of his royal status. The high priestess almost regretted that she couldn't select him to share her bed every night of the thirty day celebration. But as the king, he was only required to be there for the tenth night. And as the high priestess, she couldn't reject him, even if he was old and ugly.

Once he was naked, the priestess took a pitcher of cool, clear water and poured it over Dumuzid's body, cleansing him of the dust from his long journey. She guided the clear water with her hands, washing over his firm muscles and the ridges of his chest and back. She poured more over his head, combing her fingers through his long hair, working the dust and sweat from the tresses. She washed his beard and the back of his neck, and as she set down the empty pitcher, another full one appeared in her hands as if by magic. While the other priestesses weren't readily visible, they were still present for the sacred union, quietly making sure there was no hitch in the ritual, sending silent prayers to their goddess as they watched and worked. The high priestess continued her work, washing his flat stomach, his strong thighs, and his thick manhood. She dropped to her knees and finished with his feet, carefully wiping the skin clean with another fine piece of silk. There was the practical reason of keeping the dirt from the priestess's bed, but the bathing also symbolized the Goddesses' welcoming of her consort.

He held his hand out to her, assisting her to her feet once he was fully washed and dried. He wanted to tug the loose robes off her frame, but he'd received careful instruction before his first visit to the Temple of Eanna--the temple of Heaven. Looking at the High Priestess, he understood the name. There was much talk about the beauties and majesty of Heaven, where the sixty times sixty deities resided, but the king couldn't care less about any of that. He was a warrior with worldly goals and fixations, and the woman standing in front of him in her silk and finery was the closest thing to Heaven he could ever imagine. She was young, barely of marrying age, and she had thick, full breasts and rich curves for him to hold and sink into. He could only watch as she ever-so-slowly undressed herself, letting him catch mere glimpses of her protected and divine skin. He was vaguely aware that other people were watching, but that was only a dim consideration. She was the center of his world, the center of his attention.

When the robes fell away, she stood before him in nothing but gold and jewels. She seemed to sparkle and glow as bright as the Goddess in the sky, when she rose and set with the sun. The symbol of Ianna, the bright morning star, was fashioned out of eight magnificent diamonds and hung between her beautiful breasts. Her nipples were a shade of pink that the king had never seen before, and her body was the most inviting, alluring thing he'd never witnessed. She had wide hips and a thick thatch of hair between the marble columns of her thighs, and her hair hung down to her waist in dark, loose waves. He dropped to his knees as though he was really looking upon the Goddess, and when she touched his cheek, he didn't feel like King Sargon, the gardener turned ruler turned king, but like Dumuzid, the shepherd turned king turned consort. And he was staring up at the Goddess who gave his life purpose.

She guided him to his feet with a gentle touch to his shoulder, and they moved to the bed together. The priestesses sighed as one as they sank into the mattress and his member grew to its full length, sliding against her soft thighs. He knew he was there for only one purpose, but he couldn't quite stop himself from exploring the rest of her body. She was so soft everywhere-- softer than anything he ever felt in his own world--and his fingers danced over her skin with pure delight. His mouth followed his touch, and he kissed her throat, her breasts, her nipples, and her stomach. He kissed her hips and the creases where her thighs met her fertile valley. He buried his face between her thighs, inhaling the unbelievable, heady scent of her womanhood. It was the sweetest perfume, better than any feasts, perfumes, blossoms that he ever encountered. It was pure and earthy, reminding him of his former life and his current glories at the same time.

He licked her soft flesh--softer than the silk they were lying on--lapping up the nectar that tasted even better than it smelled. She opened her legs wider, arching her hips up in silent encouragement. His tongue grew bolder, applying more pressure, lingering longer, searching for more. He flicked the tip over her little nub of flesh, knowing that was the secret to tasting more of her sweet juices. Then he moved lower, seeking the source itself, pushing his tongue deep into her channel. Her shocked cry of pleasure echoed off the temple's stone ceiling and walls, making him clench and ache for more of the sound. He gripped her hips, fingers sinking into her giving flesh, and pushed his tongue into her again, wiggling as deeply as he could go. His mouth was bathed in her sweet taste, her juices flowing over his tongue. She cried out again, her legs closing around him with surprising strength. His manhood twitched and jerked with new excitement, and he felt torn between equally strong desires. He wanted to join with her completely, but he couldn't get enough of her nectar, and when would he have a chance to taste anything so divine again? Not even his best wine could compare to her. She was even more intoxicating.

She combed her fingers through his damp hair again and again, her nails scraping over his scalp. He stopped paying attention to the gesture until she curled her fingers without warning and yanked on his hair, pulling even closer to her pussy. She moved her hips, grinding herself into his face while his tongue slid in and out, in and out, miming what he would do to her with his thicker shaft. She pulsed around his mouth, her heartbeat racing as fast as his. She tasted fresh and pure, like he was the only man who had ever lain with her, though he obviously knew that wasn't the case. The more she moved against him, rocking and grinding, the harder he got, the more he ached to impale her and pound her into the bed.

"It's time," she finally said between harsh breaths. He murmured a small prayer of thanks because he thought he was going to burst. He'd never been so hard, so ready to take what was meant to be his. He rose above her, ready to sheath himself with another prayer of thanks, but she put a hand on his chest, stopping him. "Lie down."

He had no choice but to comply. There he was not King Sargon, he was the faithful lover of the most powerful Goddess in the land. So he settled on his back and he didn't protest when she moved above him, straddling his hips.

The priestess looked down at her new consort with a gleam in her eyes. She liked this one. Much had been rumored about King Sargon after he disposed of Ur-Zababa the previous year, but she'd seen enough to know that it was best to discard most of what was heard there at the Temple. But he was everything he was said to be and more. She settled herself more comfortably atop him and gazed down with unabashed lust at his beautiful body. He seemed like he could be a deity himself, perhaps even Dumuzid returned in the flesh. There was very little known about him, though, except that he was sometimes referred to as The Gardener, and he displaced the former king with brutal efficiency that made it clear the gods were on his side.

She dragged her attention away from him for a brief moment. Only long enough to scan the room and find the eyes watching her from the shadows and the corners. Most of the girls there were virgins, too young or inexperienced to participate in the festivals and rituals involving sacred marriages. But they were more than curious, considering it an honor, duty, obligation, and reward to watch their High Priestess couple with her consort. The young man who had acted as Dumuzid for the previous nine nights was a beautiful specimen who did very well for the most part, but he seemed like a mere child compared to the bull she now had between her legs.

"Are you ready?" He asked with a heated look in his eye.

In answer, she rose up to her knees and reached behind her, seeking out his thick shaft. The comparison to a bull was apt, and a fresh wave of desire washed through her, her entire body tingling with anticipation. Her pussy clenched and she relaxed herself before she guided the thick head to her channel. His mouth thinned and she could see the amount of willpower he was using to remain still. She appreciated his self-control, and decided she was going to do everything she could to break that self-control and make him cry out to her for mercy. In the end, that was the true purpose of this ritual--to remind the kings that they were still servants, to show them how easy it would be to break and bend them. Ultimately, to show them their power was a boon granted to them.

She braced herself on his broad chest, rose up and when she sank down, she felt his thick shaft push at her swollen, aroused flesh. She rocked back, taking in more and more of him, until she was completely seated and clenching around him. His hands went right to her hips and tensed, as if trying to make her move, but she resisted him, gripping his wrists and gently removing his hands from her body.

She laced her fingers through his and lifted herself to her knees, rising to his crown and then dropping back down. He grunted, his fingers tightening around hers, their grips becoming increasingly, equally painful. The more she moved, the tighter they held each other, though his strength was far superior to hers. The pain drove her onward instead of prompting her to retreat, fueling the rapid rise and fall of her hips as she rode him through greater and greater waves of pleasure.

The ultimate prize was held just out of her reach, though. She moved harder and faster, chasing the tail of the tiger but never quite capable of grasping it. She pushed harder, her body becoming a frenzy of movement, fueled by hunger and willpower and the mighty power of Ianna. Pure joy rose up in her, nothing more complex than the bliss that came with the act. This was her greater calling, the reason she first traveled to the Temple, and the reason she was called to be Ianna's first servant in the Temple. She not only fully enjoyed the act, she considered it to be Ianna's greatest blessing to the world, and the joy that elevated her heart felt like a personal blessing from the Goddess herself.

The king was a worthy partner, meeting her stroke for stroke, following her lead but never trying to wrest the control from her. She was most impressed that she didn't exhaust him within minutes. Even the youngest, strongest bulls lost control with her, but his strength was measured, and she could see the determination in his eyes. He would not let her beat him. A fresh surge of desire flowed through her, an excitement that couldn't be matched, as she realized she was staring down at her equal. He never backed down, never missed a beat, and did not disappoint her as she began her upward spiral towards the universe's highest point, the pinnacle of Ianna's satisfaction and pleasure.

Without releasing his hand, she brought her fingers to her slick, throbbing flesh. Her thumb brushed over her rigid nub, and she nearly doubled over because it felt so good. He didn't miss her sudden twitch, as if somebody had stabbed her with a sharp point, and the second moment of contact was with his thumb as he flicked her with the pad. She whimpered, and he responded by doing it again. Her second whimper was a moan and her muscles clamped down around him, drawing an answering moan from deep in his chest. Soon they were echoing each other, a moan for a moan, a whimper for a whimper, as they danced and spiraled around each other. He pushed on her nub harder and she slammed down with more force, angling so each thrust would hit that most tender spot inside.

"Oh...IANNA!" Her final shout was a supplication, a song, a warning, a question, and finally the only expression of pure joy that she could possibly muster. Her body was like an exploding star, light bursting from her eyes and her mouth as she felt the full glory of her Goddess fill her. She forced her eyes open so she could look at her partner, and he seemed to be transformed into a man from an ancient past, a king and shepherd who had the audacity to fall in love with a goddess. His face contorted and his shaft jerked against her tender walls, his seed spilling into the chalice of her body, completing the ritual.

They collapsed together in ragged silence, both of them breathing hard and blinking, trying to process what had just happened to them. The other priestesses kept a respectful distance, only venturing forward to help clean and dress the worn out surrogates when the high priestess beckoned them forward with a gesture of her eyes.

"This will be a good year," she whispered, an announcement as well as a vow.

6 THE ROMAN SLAVE GIRL

Quintus paused as he stepped into the bath, surprised by the unexpected sight before him. Livia, his goddess of a wife, stood in the waist deep water, looking like his own personal Aphrodite in the rising steam. Her glorious red hair fell down her back in fat ringlets, drops of water rolled down her creamy skin, and her head was back and eyes closed, while a girl Quintus didn't recognize gently scraped water from her mistress's perfect breasts.

There hadn't been talk of adding a new girl to the household, and Quintus had the feeling that the lovely little country rose had been an impulse purchase. He had no doubt that she was from outside the city walls. Her complexion was ruddy from hours spent in the sun, and her hair was the shade of sand at the rim of the blue sea. Unlike her mistress, she knew he was there. He saw the brief flicker of her honey-colored eyes in his direction before she quickly remembered her place.

"Hello my beautiful wife."

Her eyes flew open and she smiled widely, her pleasure at seeing him plain on her lovely face. "Husband, you're home. It's been so lonely here without you."

"But I see you've found yourself company."

"Oh, this is Paulina. Do you like her?"

"She's exquisite. Where did you find her?"

"Porcia acquired her when her brother died, but she couldn't afford to keep her in the household, and I told her I could find some use for her here." Livia held her arms out as he approached, his robe unbuckled and dropped from his shoulders. He stepped into the cool pool of water with a sigh of relief, the tension from his long journey and the heat from the day leaving him as he submerged himself. The only thing better was stepping into his wife's welcoming embrace, letting her arms close around him while he sought out her mouth, claiming her lips in a hard, hungry kiss. They'd been apart for far too long, and he was already hard and aching for her tender attentions. "Did I do good?"

She asked against his lips.

"You did very good, my darling. She's an amazing present to come home to."

"May I watch you take her, my lord?"

He smiled, not-so-secretly thrilled by the question. "Oh, you're such a dirty little thing, aren't you?"

"No, my lord. It's only that I get so much pleasure from seeing you pleased."

"And how would you like me to take her? Should I fuck her tight little cunt? Or is it her ass you'd like to see violated?"

Livia caught her breath at the question, her smile suddenly sly, matching his. "She's never had anybody in the ass. From what I understand, Portia's brother was saving that treat for a special occasion. It's too bad Marcus's sword had other plans, isn't it?"

"Too bad for him, but not for me." He stepped away from Livia, turning his attention back to the girl who had silently listened to the entire exchange. She quickly looked away, pointing her eyes to the water, but he already saw the trepidation in their depths. He waded through the water to stand behind her, skimming his hands down her arms and then over her torso, as if she was a horse he was considering the purchase of. She seemed healthy and felt strong. She had an overall healthy look, and he imagined she'd been well fed and treated with some regard in her former home. His prick sat up at attention, eagerly nudging against her ass while he continued his physical examination.

"Have you had her?" He asked conversationally.

"I've used her mouth. It was nice."

"Hmm, I would like to see that. Come, sit on the edge of the pool."

Livia did as he instructed, spreading her legs wide while he guided the girl's head down. He pushed her face into Livia's wet pussy, holding it there with a strong hand until she started to lap at the flesh. Livia put her hands behind her and leaned back, her mouth falling open as Paulina focused on the core of her womanly pleasure, lapping at the hard nub jutting from her perfectly bald mound.

"Fuck her with your tongue," Quintus ordered. The girl obeyed, shifting her attention to his wife's hot entrance, her tongue plunging in without hesitation. Livia's hand came down on her head, and she held the girl's face in place, humping her hips against the tongue invading her heat. Quintus watched with greedy eyes as the pink tongue disappeared into her dripping cunt, his cock getting harder by the second. She was bent at the waist, but he put a hand on her back and forced her lower, giving him easier access and a better view of her rounded ass. It reminded him of a piece of ripe fruit, one he wanted to sink his teeth into. He brought his hand down with a hard slap, smiling as she jumped, and the red imprint of his palm formed in sharp relief on her creamy skin. He did it again and again and again, bringing his hand down with no regard to her pain, smiling as the red imprint turned purple and then the darker blue of a bruise. Livia moaned along with each crack of skin-hitting skin, as though she could feel the blows on her own body.

"You like that?" Quintus asked.

"Oh yes," Livia moaned. "Don't stop. It feels so good."

He hit her again, this time watching his wife's pussy as the blow landed. The girl's nose drove into her clitoris, and when he did it again, he listened closely for the moan—the one she couldn't quite swallow but Livia no doubt felt vibrate through her tight channel. He shifted his attention to her other cheek, bringing his hand down in hard, rapid blows that soon had Livia crying out, her shout of pleasure following each loud crack. He beat the girl more swiftly, alternating cheeks and hands until her moans were sobs and Livia was shouting her pleasure to the top of the high marble ceiling, her pussy gushing with her pleasure. The smell of her juices, the sight of her flushed, satisfied face, was too much for him to ignore. He wasn't just hard, he was ready to burst, but he made sure she was watching before he lined his thick dick up to the slave's clenched pucker.

He spit on his fingers and wiped them over her hole to ease his way. She was still crying, though her sobs were back to their earlier silent levels her body still shook with each one. He fit his crown against the tiny opening—she didn't even look like she could take his finger much less something as thick as dick--and took her by the shoulders. Instead of thrusting forward, he pulled her back onto his shaft, using his strength and her weight to force the thick rod of meat into her oh-so-tight ass. She cried out in pain and protest, and Livia was quick to slap her face, stunning her into silence. He used more force, not relenting until she was completely impaled and his dick was buried in her bowels.

"How does it feel?" Livia cooed.

"Fucking amazing," Quintus gritted out. Her heart was pounding and her flesh was pulsing around him, her ass clenching even tighter. He'd never, ever felt anything like it and he didn't want to ever move. He didn't even want to pump his hips; he just wanted to stand there in the cool water and let her impossible heat flex around him until she simply squeezed the pleasure from him. She started to make noise again. Livia fisted her hair and slammed her face down into the water. The girl automatically struggled, her body tensing with fear, squeezing him even tighter, and every movement seemingly pushing her further back onto his shaft. When she stopped struggling, Livia lifted her head from the water and gasped for breath.

"Keep that up and I won't last very long," Quintus warned.

"That's fine, darling. We have all night with her after all." Livia plunged her head in the water again. This time, there wasn't an immediate struggle. Not until the seconds ticked by and her lungs started to burn from lack of oxygen. Then she went crazy, and his cock nearly spasmed right there, his groin pulling tight, but he managed to beat back that tide of pleasure, using all of his self-control to keep from busting in her ass.

"Fuck her," Livia urged, lifting her face from the water and letting her breathe again. "Pound her."

His grin was wolfish, "With pleasure."

His grip was bruising on her shoulders, and he arched his hips back, slowly easing back from the impossibly tight sheath of her ass before slamming forward. Her shout of pain was half muffled by water as Livia plunged her head back down. Livia was strong, and she only had to use one hand to keep her head under water as Quintus set a brutal pace. He knew he was hurting her and could feel her skin give and tear beneath his forceful thrusts. He had to move fast because he knew exactly what was going to happen, and at this point, it was a race against time itself. Her pulse pounded harder than before as her fear spiked and her body clenched even tighter as the darkness fell down on her.

One second she was struggling and the next she was completely lax. The charge that set off was instant and his balls pulled tight, and he buried himself deep in her body and erupted. Livia pulled her face from the water and wrapped his arms around her, squeezing her chest hard enough to force the water from her lungs. It took two attempts, but the water erupted from her lungs and she coughed herself awake, sputtering and gasping while his cock jerked in her ass, the aftershocks of his pleasure still rolling down his spine. He looked down, noticing that her thighs were covered in pink water—water that only darkened as he pulled his dick free of her tight channel.

"Just what I needed." He gripped Livia by the back of the neck and pulled her down into a kiss. "Now I can fuck my darling wife properly. You must have been very lonely without me here."

"Oh yes, my lord. A mouth is nice but..." She reached between them and gripped his softening shaft. A single squeeze of her fingers and he was getting hard again. She really was like a Goddess to him, his body constantly on high alert around her and always immediately responsive. "This is what I really needed. Don't make me wait for it, darling, please."

"Of course not." He quickly washed his shaft of any evidence of his coupling with the slave and then took Livia by the hips, angling upwards while he pulled her down on his shaft. They met with a mutual sigh of relief, her legs wrapping around him while her liquid heat soaked into his flesh. He grunted, thrusting into her in the hard, short rhythm that she preferred. Her heels dug into his ass, her fingernails scratching up and down his back while he jerked his hips, the base of his cock slamming hard into her clitoris. He lost track of the slave, forgetting that there was anybody there but him and his beloved wife.

He'd been called to do business in Rome, taking him away from home for over a month. He'd been well entertained by his host, a veritable parade of girls and boys brought before him for his pleasure. He didn't have a single appetite that didn't go well fed and satisfied, but none of them could satisfy him like Livia. She knew exactly how to move, exactly how to kiss him and scratch him and when to bite him and how to urge him into more. The difference between her and the rest of them was that she was a real partner to him, an equal in surprising and wonderful ways.

"Do you want to fuck the girl again?"

"Not as much as I want to keep fucking you. But I do plan to have her again."

"When you're done with her, throw her down to the gladiators. I'm sure they'll be grateful for the scraps."

"If there's enough of her left to share," Quintus promised, though he couldn't say for sure there would be. As Livia already pointed out herself, they still had all night ahead of them, and even though Livia was riding him with all she had, he knew he was just getting started. Their mouths met again, flames erupting from the heat and force of the caress. Their tongues dueled, a million promises flowing between them with every second. He could read her so well that he sensed when the quality of her kisses changed, when her lips became more demanding and her mouth changed shape with the shout she was trying to hold back.

"Or maybe we can bring a few of the bulls up here for the night," Quintus whispered in her ear. "Let them put on a show for you. How does that sound?"

She didn't speak, but she didn't have to.

The sudden clenching in her body and the way her eyes rolled back in her head was all the answer he needed. He rode out her orgasm, moving his hips even faster as her cum coated him in slick liquid. Water splashed all over them and the tiles, and he felt hot liquid roll down his back—it must have been blood from the crescent-shaped marks she left with her nails. He fisted her long hair and pulled hard enough to shock her into a third spiral, and this time, her hips rolled with so much force that he couldn't withstand. As her pleasure reverberated through her, he shot his load for the second time, pumping his seed deep into his wife's womb.

7 MARRYING THE WOLF

There was only one woman Gorlacon would have for a queen once he united the scattered tribes of Picts into one kingdom under his rule. She was Etain, a wolf who wanted nothing to do with men, a tracker, a hunter, and a warrior. She was made of men's nightmares, and there was no escaping her vengeance. There was fierceness and grace in every movement, and his admiration for her was boundless. He had no desire to subdue her or trap her, but he did want her at his side and in his bed – if only for a single night. Still, if she wouldn't agree to even one night, there were other ways to slake his thirst, and he would still have her at his side. He didn't doubt he could have her. He rose up from a farmer to a king because nobody in the land could fight better. If it was a matter of will and strength, then he was well suited to the task.

Etain came and went as she pleased. The longest she'd ever stay was two nights.

She'd always be gone by the third morning, and where she went, why she went there, and when she would return were all mysteries belonging to the gods. He never asked, only made room for her, and treated her as an honored guest when she returned. One night after a visit, his men were being particularly obnoxious in their speculations, especially since once of the spies saw her among the Romans in their garrison on the disputed border. Gorlacon stabbed the man in the throat before he could say another word and gave the audience a hard stare, daring them to say another word. Nobody mentioned Etain again until she came riding in camp with her flinty stare, her unknowable mind working in its unknowable ways.

Gorlacon knew why she went to the Romans. She was hunting. Mute since a young age, the Romans were responsible for her rape and subsequent loss of her tongue.

When she passed herself off as a cast out, she was lulling them into a false sense of security, slowly enticing them to her final trap. She didn't tell him any of this, and she wouldn't have even if she could speak, but he still knew, because the two of them were of the same kind. She became the wolf when Roman soldiers violated and essentially killed the child, but Gorlacon knew one thing above all else – she was always the wolf. He was one, too. And they were destined to rule together and turn the Romans pack, push them all the way back to their own lands, and then take those as well.

When his spies reported that Etain had been spotted riding toward their camp, Gorlacon took advantage of the rare chance to anticipate her arrival. He recruited his two most loyal men and went through the preparations of his wedding, including a hunting trip to secure enough venison for their celebration, and a fresh hide for his wedding bed. By the time she arrived, he was dressed in his best gear, his blades polished, and his quiver full and strapped to his back. He mounted his black stallion and met her, warrior to warrior. There was curiosity in her eyes but no fear, and she watched as he approached; his hands open and out so she could see he meant her no harm.

"Etain, you are the best warrior in the land and my only true equal." There was a rumble among the men, but nobody stepped forward to protest. No doubt they were all aware she'd be happy to defend her new title. "It is only right that you share the duties and glory of ruling the people you fight for."

In all the time he knew her, he never saw her surprised. Even the most well executed secret attacks never caught her off guard because nothing stayed a secret from her for very long. But her eyes were wide, and for the first time, the deadly wolf mask slipped away, revealing there was still a woman somewhere inside of her.

He dismounted from his horse and moved to her side, putting his arms up so he could lift her – or catch her.

"Please, Etain, do me the honor of being my queen."

She tilted her head, her face slowly settling back to the mask he knew so well. She considered him for long seconds, perhaps weighing her options, before giving a slight shake of her head.

Gorlacon wasn't discouraged.

"You will not be chained down to my side, Etain. You will be allowed to do as you please since this land will be yours and all on it subject to your whims. I need a queen and you are the one I would have."

She moved her arms in front of her chest, as if cradling a baby, and shook her head.

"I have a son. I do not have a queen. If

you would rather keep your own bed, then I will accept that."

Her eyes were slits of silver, as unreadable and flat as the moon. If she wouldn't have him now, he knew that she wouldn't have him at all. He was giving her all he had, and asking her nothing in return and his feelings and esteem for her were so high that this seemed like a fair trade to him. Even if she would not have him, she would be loyal to him and fight for him and what couldn't he conquer with her at his side? He didn't mention any of that because she knew it – and if she didn't, then maybe she shouldn't be his queen after all.

After what felt like an eternity, she inclined her head slightly and placed her hands on his shoulders, allowing him to lift her from her horse. There was nothing soft about her body, and when he pulled her against him, holding her for the space of a heartbeat, she didn't feel much like a woman. He guided her away from the center of camp, through the throngs of cheering men who gathered to watch the transaction, and into the privacy of his personal tent. His hunters had brought back a half-dozen deer, and their scraped hides now adorned his bed. He would have it cured into leather and made into new clothes for her if she preferred.

She began to undress, taking him by

surprise. It seemed as though she was discarding her thick pelt, once again allowing him to see the woman who still existed in the wolf. As her leather and armor fell away, it was easy to see that while she didn't feel soft, she was an amazingly beautiful woman. He longed to touch her, but knowing she could still kill him, even naked and unarmed, stayed his hand. She pointed to the thatch of hair between her legs, and then pointed to her stomach and shook her head before once again miming holding a baby and giving another shake.

"You'll have me but there will never be a child?"

She nodded and then lowered herself to the fresh hides, looking up at him with quiet expectance. He'd thought about this so many times that now he couldn't quite believe it was happening and not just another dream. Even in his dreams, it was never this easy. Could she still have a weapon on her somewhere? Perhaps what he took as mutual respect was only his wishful thinking, and she always planned to kill him and take his title. On the other hand, she could have killed him and claimed his title at any time. That was how he earned the crown, after all. With that in mind, he began to undress himself, taking away his own pelt so she could see the man underneath. He watched for her reaction, though, as expected, she gave nothing away.

He had a hard body, hewn from a hard life that never allowed him a moment of respite. She was largely, surprisingly, unscarred, but he wore every battle on his skin; some scars faded almost to nothing, and others still fresh enough to be red, each one a source of pride. They announced to the world that he'd earned his position and his power. He knelt beside her, and she ghosted her fingers over the scars on his chest, following their twisted, uneven lines from one to the other until her hand traveled from his neck to his groin. Her touch was surprisingly gentle; without a single hint of the death she dealt out on a regular basis. He held himself still, wanting to touch her in return, but unwilling to do anything to startle her. She continued on, learning the marks on his thighs, his hips, then up his ribs, and over his back. She seemed to be searching for something, but he didn't know what. She dragged her calloused fingers down to his wrist and then took his hand, guiding his palm to her breast. He didn't know what to call the feeling that surged through him at the first touch. It was something he normally associated with the victory of battle, with the warm spray of his enemy's blood across his face as he hacked and slashed through the falling defenses. He'd never felt it like this, though. He massaged the small buds of her breasts, palming them and squeezing gently. She sighed softly and he felt that strange sensation again. He already wanted her, but now his desire reached a new peak. Knowing he could have her after all made him achingly aroused. Her nipples tightened and he lowered his head to slide his tongue over the tip, tasting the salt and the sky on her skin. Other women tasted and smelled like the cooking fire, but she rarely slept inside a tent let alone stood over an open flame to prepare food.

He was so caught up in the taste and smell of her that he didn't notice she was moving until he was on his back and she was straddling him. She pressed her lips to his in a hard kiss before moving down his body, leaving a trail of bite marks as she went. Her teeth were sharp and she was not gentle, biting hard enough to draw blood in a few cases. He could only stare as she left her mark on him, claiming him so that all could see that he belonged to the wolf. The bites bloomed into bloody bruises, each one a small circle the perfect size and shape of her mouth. Her lips twitched into something like a smile, and she rubbed her fingers across the growing drops of blood, smearing them over his skin. She moved her fingers in fluid motions, painting a series of designs on his chest, pressing on the wounds, and forcing more blood from the teeth marks when she ran out. He looked down, but in the dim light of the tent, he couldn't quite see what she was doing. It didn't matter though because her touch felt amazing, every bit of coming alive once her light fingers moved over him, soothing away the hurt, marking him in an entirely new way. She smoothed her hands down her chest, spreading his blood in uneven streaks down her unmarred skin. She dropped down; her chest sliding against tender, bruised skin; and he felt all of her bites again, all at once. The pain burned through him, but he'd felt worse on the battlefield, and it did nothing to lessen his desire. She rocked back and forth, smearing the blood over both of them, and kissed him again, attacking his mouth with her teeth. He didn't bite her back and didn't resist or turn his head. She seemed to have a message with each bite, and he thought he understood. Being with her was going to be painful. It was going to hurt, and she would make him bleed because she liked the sight and the feel of his blood. Could he accept that?

He could.

He would.

He did.

She rose up again, giving him a good

view of his blood on her skin. She slid his cock between her thighs, and he was a little surprised to feel that she was more than ready for him. Her opening was hot and slick, and it took everything he had not to slam his hips upward, not to flip her on her back and drill into her. But this wasn't just about his satisfaction. He could treat any of the women in his camp, yet it was this woman he chose. She sank back, taking him slowly, pausing occasionally, and simply breathing, while he trembled and strained and yearned for more. Her hands still traveled up and down his skin, like she couldn't get enough of the feel of blood.

Finally, he was completely inside of her. She sat straight up and took him by the shoulders, pulling him up to meet her. With their mouths even, she kissed him again, her legs wrapping around his waist. He wrapped his arms around her, holding her as tight as he could. He always thought their coupling, should it ever happen, would be as frenzied and frantic as a battle. He expected somebody to bleed, but he never thought he would simply hold her against him, while she wrapped around him tighter than anybody else ever had. They weren't completely still. Their hips moved in increments, their bodies clenched, and their muscles contracted and jerked. Every tiny motion and twitch sent a cascade of chills down his spine, each time more powerful than the one before it until he couldn't take it anymore and he had to move.

He rolled them over, pinning her back to the bed. She immediately tensed and tried to fight him, her hands like bird talons flying toward his face. He caught her wrists and brought her hands above her head, holding them both within one large hand.

She stared up at him with cold defiance, ready to tear his face off, ready to kill him.

He didn't understand how she could turn so quickly, and he didn't know how to turn off her anger or at least divert it.

"Etain...Etain it's me. It's me. I'm not going to hurt you, Etain. I'm not going to do anything to harm you. I'm your husband now."

The words seemed to have some impact, so he kept talking until the fight melted from her. He felt the difference in her body, and he tentatively released her wrists and moved his hips. She moaned, her eyes fluttering closed, and he knew it would be okay. He moved his hips in the same way, sliding into her, thrusting deep before easing out again. He kept it slow and avoided using any real strength. He didn't move faster until she did, grunting softly and slotting her hips forward, rising to meet him. They fell into a matching rhythm, rutting against each other with increasing speed, their silence only occasionally punctuated by gasps and moans. When he felt himself getting close, he touched the side of her face, urging her to open her eyes. It was dark but the silver discs caught what little light was in the tent and sent it reflecting back – another reminder that she was a wolf. He wasn't afraid though and didn't look away. He wanted to see her the moment he claimed her with his seed. She stared back, her face flickering as the pleasure increased. Her walls clenched around him and he wanted more, wanted to keep moving, but suddenly she was shaking and mewing, and the sudden pressure around his shaft was too much for him. He flooded her with his pleasure, covering her faces with tiny kisses as he pumped his seed deep inside.

They collapsed together, and though he needed to wash and there was food to offer, he didn't want to move. Outside his tent, his men kept a constant lookout for the Romans, while the stars spun overhead. They would be safe. They could rest together for a short while before venturing away from the heat for the ice of battle.

8 THE CENTURION'S MESSAGE

Septus fought his way through bitter cold, snow, and ice with blood flowing freely down his chest, knowing he had to keep his feet moving; forcing himself forward with nothing fueling him but sheer will. The last time he ate was the morning before the Goths' attack, and that was four, maybe five days ago. He tried to keep moving during the day, but once he woke up in an open space with no memory of falling asleep, and he had no idea how long he was passed out there. He hadn't let himself rest for two days now, knowing that if he stopped, he would never get moving again. But the Seventh Regiment was garrisoned to the south, and he needed to make his report before he let himself rest. Then if he met his end, at least he would go to Hades knowing he'd fulfilled his promise and maybe even be saved and lived.

On the third day since he passed out, there were no clouds in the sky, and the sky glared brightly off the endless sheets of snow, blinding him. He stumbled on through the icy crust, slipping and barely catching himself, lurching through the depths. He strained his ears, trying to use them to guide him on, but there was nothing to be heard. Or maybe the snow muffled everything. His nose twitched at what might have been faint wood smoke, and his heart lurched with hope. His foot caught on a root at that moment, sending him headfirst into the snow. He barely had the strength to move it away from his mouth, let alone stand up again. If he fell asleep there, he knew that would be it. He'd die probably no more than a few miles from the garrison and his message would die with him. When the Goths descended, there'd be no warning and the Garrison would be outnumbered and caught off guard this late in the winter.

When he heard the familiar rhythm of an approaching horse, he didn't dare hope it was anything more than a dream, or perhaps the sound of his own death. He hoped it was the former as he submitted to the darkness.

"Wake up, Septus. Otherwise I'll eat your rations and you'll go hungry for another day."

The words barely made sense, but the voice came to him from the past, reaching through the years to yank him out of the comfortable darkness. He opened his eyes slowly, blinking to clear the fog from his vision as Macros's face came into view. "How can this be? Am I dead?"

Macros laughed. "Of course you're not dead. But it was a very close thing. I have some delicious gruel for you."

"Where am I?"

"Seventh garrison."

Septus's eyes widened and he sat straight up, his exhaustion forgotten, his delight at seeing his old friend chilling to a familiar dread. "Who's in charge here? I must speak to him."

"General Titus Virilus. But you need to eat first."

"It's urgent. The Goths are planning an attack. They already obliterated the Ninth." He gripped his old friend's arm. "Listen to me, Macros. I'm all that's left of three thousand men. And they're still on the march."

"I'll report to the general right now, and I'll tell him everything you told me, but you need to remain here and eat." Macros pushed the bowl into his hands. "You have my rations as well. But eat slowly."

"Macros..."

"Eat. If what you say is true then we're going to need every single man to pick up a sword and that includes you. You're no good to me dead."

Septus couldn't argue and he trusted Macros to deliver his message. He obediently lifted the spoon to his mouth, earning a small but achingly familiar smile from him before he ducked out of the room. They'd once been inseparable, both the sons of gladiators, both joining the legion on their fifteenth birthdays, which they also shared. They'd been closer than brothers for five years, fighting at each other's sides and emerging with their lives intact after each battle--often due to the other's interference at a crucial moment. Septus knew he could lose Macros at any time, but he always expected it to be in bloody battle, and he always expected he would die shortly after his partner. It seemed inevitable. But instead of dying at his side, Macros had simply disappeared. Septus had assumed he'd never see his friend again and mourned, though he never fully got over the loss. How could he be with the Seventh now? What had happened to him? And what Gods brought them together again? He never said prayers for Macros because he never knew what to say.

He had time to finish both servings and drink from the pitcher of water left before Macros returned. Septus tried to stand to greet him, but his legs were too weak and Macros gently pushed him back to the bed, leaving his hand on Septus's chest until he settled on his back. "You need to rest."

"What did he say?" Septus asked.

"He's preparing for the attack. Now relax. You've done everything you could."

"I thought you were dead."

Macros sighed. "I nearly was. The Goths captured me but I escaped before they killed me. Eventually I found the Seventh but there was no way to get a message to you. Perhaps that was the Gods way to ensure I'd be here when you needed me."

"Did you find me?"

"Yes. You were so near death I feared you wouldn't wake again. But you've always had a strong spirit."

"I'm the only one who survived. I had a duty."

"You were always the most honorable man I ever knew. How are you feeling? I'm sure the General would be happy to allow you another bowl."

"I am full, thank you." His stomach had already cramped once and he definitely didn't want to lose it all before it had the chance to do any good.

"What about your injury?"

Septus looked down at his freshly bandaged chest. He touched it gingerly, feeling for the inflammation and soreness of an infection, but it seemed clean; tender but not alarmingly so.

"Is this your work?"

"Like I would let anybody else near you."

"You've gotten better."

"Unfortunately, I've had a lot of practice. Not too many men have my steady hand when it gets this cold."

Septus didn't think that would be a problem this time--because the Goths didn't intend to leave any survivors. He hid under a heap of dead bodies for two days, unable to block the smell of decomposition, staunching the blood from his chest wound with whatever spare scrap of cloth he could tear off the bodies. He made his escape under the cover of darkness, hoping to find some sign of a survivor, but he never came across another set of tracks.

"I expected it to be worse. But that was your only wound and it was shallow."

"I hid." The words were shameful but he said them anyway because Macros wouldn't judge him.

"And because of that, you're here to warn us now. The Gods..."

"Stop. If the Gods cared so much, why

don't they help us bring an end to these barbarians? Why allow the destruction of an entire garrison?"

"It's not for us to know."

"That's bullshit."

"I missed you."

Septus swallowed around the sudden stiffness in his throat and moved to the edge of the bed, making room for Macros to join him. Macros looked at him, but made no move. Septus felt a flare of panic but dampened it and held himself still, unflinchingly meeting his gaze. Maybe things had changed too much. Maybe Macros was a different person now. But Septus knew they were living on borrowed time and he wanted to know the comfort of Macros's familiar, beloved body once more before his second meeting with the Goths. Something changed on Macros's face the moment his decision was made, and he began to disrobe. Soon he was wearing nothing but the low orange glow from the candle, and there was only enough light to see his outline--broad shoulders, narrow hips, sharp profile and curly hair. Septus didn't need to see the details. He knew those already.

He settled on the bed and pulled the blanket over their heads, shutting out the world entirely, creating a cocoon big enough to house only them. Septus sighed and curled as close as he could, resting his head on Macros's shoulder, feeling warm for the first time since...well, the first time since the day he lost Macros. The chill in his flesh and his heart were both chased away. They had spent countless nights sleeping this way, and it was a joy that Septus believed he would never experience again.

Macros shifted, turning onto his side so they were face-to-face, groin-to-groin. A new fire kindled in his belly as soon as his cock touched the other man's, and he grew to his full length, the crown nudging against Macros's thigh. He moved to take a hold of himself, but Macros beat him to it, wrapping his long fingers around both of them. His skin was smoother, softer, than anything Septus ever felt, and he whimpered as Macros flexed his fingers, squeezing their cocks together. He could feel Macros's pulse throbbing through his flesh, and his heart sped up in response. Desire and need melted together and poured through his system, and he needed more. He needed to be closer, to feel Macros throbbing all around him and below him.

"I need you," Septus whispered. "I know...we didn't...but I need to be with you." He hoped Macros understood, but more than that, he hoped Macros realized there would be no shame in it. Not this time. Not when they were full of mutual need and this could very well be their last night on earth.

Without saying a word, Macros released their shafts and rolled onto his stomach, silently offering what Septus was too afraid to ask for by name. He lifted his leg over Macros's hips and lay over his back, kissing the soft part of his neck and across his shoulders. He couldn't see the shape or placement of the new scars, but he could feel them. He knew--or he once knew--Macros's body better than he knew his own, and there were new marks there, new stories Septus would never hear about battles that now meant nothing.

He lifted his head from the blanket and looked around the small bunk, spotting the bottle of oil and the scraper. He poured most of what was left in the bottle into his palm and over his shaft, slicking himself and his fingers. He dipped his fingers between his twin moons to find the pucker. The muscle gave easily to Septus's probing, slick finger, and he pushed all the way up to his knuckle, working in and out a few times before adding a second finger. He listened closely for any sign of discomfort, but Macros didn't make a single sound. Septus kissed him again and again while he pumped his wrist, his lips drawn to the textured mystery of his skin. His need had been so great that it forced the question he'd never asked before, and he thought that was the upper boundary. But he'd been wrong. His hunger grew by the second until his whole world had narrowed down to one single thought.

That was when he adjusted himself over Macros's supine form, his cock pointed straight down to his target. All he had to do was thrust his hips forward and let himself sink right into the heat. He felt like he was falling, moving in slow motion until his injured chest came to a rest on Macros's back. He braced himself with his hands on either side of Macros and buried his face in the other man's neck, breathing in his scent--so familiar that it was like he never missed it, but the sharp pang in his chest reminded him that an important piece had been missing from his life.

He took his time, thrusting down with lethargic precision. The morning would come soon enough; he didn't need to rush it. He wanted every second to last all night, convinced it couldn't get any better even though it never stopped getting better. He wanted Macros to make a sound, wanted to know that he was feeling the same heat, the same endless spirals of pleasure.

"Gods," Macros finally choked out, and

there was more meaning in that single word than in a library of learned scrolls. Septus heard the world in his voice, and that moment, that single reaction, felt like his reward for fighting and surviving. It was like a sudden sword to the heart, the sudden sensation so profound that Septus forgot he didn't even believe in the Gods anymore. How could he doubt when he found this happiness at the end of his life? He wasn't angry that he only had a short time to know this bliss--he never thought he would know it at all. A second of it was as invaluable as a lifetime, and the seconds kept accumulating, bringing him closer and closer to his final release.

He grabbed Macros by the hair and forced his head back, claiming his mouth with a kiss as hard as a punch. Macros immediately parted his lips, challenge accepted, met, and then extended. No matter how hard Septus kissed him, Macros returned the kiss with exceeding fervor. Soon their hips were moving with the passion of their kisses, and though Septus wanted to take it slow, he couldn't hold himself back. He moved faster, slamming down harder, and Macros went from near silence to grunting with each powerful thrust. Septus unconsciously echoed him, until the sounds were closer to shouts and they had to fuse their mouths to muffle the sounds and avoid waking the whole garrison.

When he felt himself getting close to the end, he shifted back to his knees, gripping Macros by the hips and pulling him up off the bed. He slammed him back, taking advantage of their better position to dig deep and find the last of his strength. He slid his hand around Macros's hips and fisted his cock, stroking his length in time with the pounding of his hips. He held himself back, waiting, trying to time it because he wanted to feel his friend's pleasure before he lost himself to his own. Just when he thought he wouldn't be able to last for another stroke, Macros's cock jerked in his hand, shooting sticky strings into his palm. As soon as the fluid touched him, he was lost, his cock jerking wildly within the sheath of Macros's ass.

When he was completely spent, his exhaustion returned like a slap to the face and he couldn't stop himself from literally collapsing, falling back to the bed with a thud, his eyes already closed. He wanted nothing more than to curl up in Macros's arms, but the other man moved off the bed. He heard him moving around the small room, and then he felt a slightly damp rag move over his groin, wiping away the mess. He felt the rim of the cup press to his lips and he opened them to accept the fresh water. He knew nothing was moving but everything was spinning.

Taking Macros like that had probably sapped the last of his strength--it was the exact opposite of resting. But he had no regrets. Not for his final night on earth.

9 A NECESSARY ALLIANCE

Queen Imogen had been born in a den of vipers, forced by necessity to learn wiles and deceit at a young age. She understood that to beat her treacherous family at their own game and win the power for herself, she had to produce a male heir because she would never be able to claim the throne in her own name. Consequently, she was an eager participant in her marriage bed, even though she'd been married off at a young age. But no matter how many times she laid with her husband, she couldn't conceive a child. She consulted her ladies-in-waiting, and they gently pointed out that their king was old—old enough to have a nearly grown son—and perhaps the problem is with him. She was the same age as Prince John and should have been his bride, but the old king was selfish and clutched at everything he thought his son might want. It took longer to think of a workable plan than it did to make the decision.

Fortunately, John was a loyal subject to his father but a rather bitter and resentful son. He never crossed the king when it came to state affairs, but he seemed to take special delight in annoying his father, sometimes even thwarting or outright ignoring him. When she sent for him, ordering an audience with him late one afternoon, she knew he would answer her summons. And he did directly after his daily practice with his squadron of knights. He came in with mussed and sweaty hair, a flushed face, and a winded, satisfied look that Imogen would like to associate with other activity.

"Your Highness," John said, bending low.

"John. Please, have a seat. You look exhausted. Would you care for refreshment?"

"Yes, I'm rather famished."

Imogen gestured at the nearest servant, silently ordering her to bring in the food that she'd already ordered upstairs from the kitchen. Once the sumptuous platters were brought in and placed between them, Imogen sent all the servants away, leaving the two of them alone.

"Aren't you worried about the gossip?" John asked pointedly.

"They have nothing to gossip about. Do they?"

He shrugged and heaped food on his plate. He wasn't kidding about being starving, and he ate with an appetite appropriate for a man his age and size. He was taller than his father and broader, too, with a warrior's build. He was apparently a natural fighter, picking up his first sword as soon as he could walk. He was dangerous, a walking, talking weapon of the state. There were already whispers of potential marriages floating around the court, and she hated the thought of any of those rumors becoming reality. She didn't want to see him married off to some undeserving princess. Could she somehow delay it? Or was the old king determined to see his son wed before he died?

He talked while he ate, detailing that day's practice, giving her a rundown of the knights' strengths and weaknesses, like she personally cared. She was good at pretending she cared, though, and it was easy enough to nod her head and laugh when he said something witty or clever. When they were done eating, they moved to her salon, leaving the mess of platters behind them by tacit agreement. She made it a point to close the door behind them and John didn't miss the gesture.

"You know you're playing a dangerous game."

"What do you mean?"

"If the king finds out about this, he'll have somebody's head, either yours or mine."

"What do you think is happening?"

He gave her an exasperated look. "Don't do that. We don't have enough time. I've noticed the way you've looked at me, Imogen." That was the first time he ever addressed her by name, and she liked the sound of it. Loved the way it rolled off his tongue. "Because I've been looking at you, too. I've just been waiting for you to do something about it."

"If you've been waiting, why didn't you do something?"

"Surely, you know this has to be your idea. Even if I'm in full agreement with it."

"Even if you think the king will have your head?"

"Or yours," he reminded her. "But that seems to be a small price to pay. You certainly seem to think the risk is worth it."

"Only because I should have always been yours."

He smiled and held his hand out. "Come to your true master, then."

She folded her fingers around his and he turned her hand into his grip, yanking her against his chest. She had to crane her head back to see his eyes, and he looked down at her with smoldering eyes, the blue depths burning with desire. She figured he would be agreeable to an alliance, but she saw much more than that reflected on his face. For the first time, he was looking at her without any shields or disguises, allowing her to see passion, lust, and even...devotion? Something melted inside her chest, and she forgot all about her practical reasons for taking him into her bed. She was just a young woman—practically a girl—standing in the arms of a tall, handsome man whose eyes captivated her and whose touch didn't surprise or disgust her. She was that young woman when she lifted her chin and strained toward his kiss, meeting his mouth with a small, pleased gasp.

His hands roamed freely over her body, seeking for the weakness in her feminine armor, the point that would allow him entry past the layers of material to her flushed skin. He wore a loose tunic and soft buckskin pants that were held around his hips with a simple tie. She pulled the knot loose and let his pants fall to the floor, her hands traveling the opposite direction to bunch his tunic up around his shoulders. He yanked the material over his head, leaving him completely naked and bathed in sunlight slanting in from the window overhead. Their mouths met again and again, neither one of them willing to break contact for too long.

He scooped her off the floor, lifting her into his arms without warning and carrying her through to her bedroom. All she had to do was curl up to his rock-solid chest and she was complete wet, flooded with desire that she never felt before, even when she was watching him fight in the tournaments. But there had been plenty of distance between them, and now there was absolutely nothing separating them. No space and definitely not enough clothes to make any difference. He lowered her to the down-stuffed mattress and ripped the material off her chest. She liked the dress but she barely noticed the tear, too relieved to finally feel his long, clever fingers. She arched her back, moving into the touch while he used his other hand to finish unwrapping her. She shrugged the remnants of her dress away, her entire body burning and yearning for more of him.

She never slept with the king in her bed, choosing to go to his room when he wanted her. She was glad now that she kept such a sharp distinction between her private space and her married life. It was much easier to cradle John between her legs without being reminded of similar times with her husband. This was her first time in that bed, in that room. And in a way, she felt like this was far more momentous than her wedding night. Compared to the feelings simply looking at John evoked, her wedding night couldn't even begin to count. The first time with the king had been difficult and frightening, something to be withstood even if she was hopeful for the possible results. But she never got her result, and she never got one iota of the pleasure that John gave her by simply existing, never mind touching her body like it was something cherished and unexpected. He called himself her true master, but he didn't have the same thoughtless, entitled roughness that his father possessed.

He dipped his head and licked at her nipple, teasing it to a stiff point with the tip of his tongue. He closed his lips around the flesh and sucked. At first, she didn't feel much of anything, though the sensation of his mouth around the soft skin was vaguely pleasant. He sucked harder and she felt an answering twinge between her legs. She made a small sound of surprise, an unconscious guide for him to follow. He closed his teeth around her and the twinge between her thighs exploded, moving up her body in a sharp flare. Her gasp was louder, and he responded by adding more pressure. The sensations intensified until she was panting, begging him to stop because she couldn't take it anymore.

But he ignored her, his fingers pinching around the other nipple. He bit and pinched, sucked and caressed, and licked and massaged, alternating enough to keep her guessing, but never enough to give her a second of relief. The heat in her stomach grew brighter and hotter, and she had no concept of what was happening. Nothing to compare the experience to. Fear spiked through her, and icy shaft piercing right through her midsection, and she jerked away, hitting at his head and hand to try to make him stop.

"Hey...hey...what's going on? Are you hurt? Did I hurt you?"

"No...no, I don't think so. It's just...it feels..."

"Like it's too much?"

She nodded.

"That's how it's supposed to feel. Don't fight me, Imogen. Let me show you how good it can be."

"It's supposed to...but I never felt anything like this before," she said, sounding winded.

"I'm sure you haven't. I doubt my father

is particularly concerned about what you want. You're only here for his needs, just like the rest of us." He bent his golden head, licked her again, and then looked up through his lashes. "But I'm here for your needs, too. And I intend to see to every single one of them."

"Oh," she breathed. She didn't even know what those needs were, but she let go of her fear, turning herself over to him with complete trust. There was no doubt a long list of servants and courtesans who taught their prince everything he needed to know, and quite frankly, she heartily approved of that education. The corners of his mouth lifted in a small smile that made her heart clench quite inexplicably, and then he was sucking her nipple between his lips again.

This time, the sudden sharp pleasure between her legs didn't take her by surprise. She didn't try to fight it, either. She didn't question it or let her mind take control again. She simply turned herself over to that amazing sensation, sinking in, submerging herself so she could drown in it. He pinched, rolling the nub between his finger and thumb while he sucked hard enough to hollow his cheeks and all that pleasure surged, completely taking her over. She rose off the bed, a cry escaping from her mouth, and he slapped his hand over her lips, muffling her. She couldn't stop moaning, and she couldn't stop moving her hips. She thrust them frantically, rocking them up and down as if he already had his tool inside of her. Her thighs were wet, slick with new fluid she couldn't explain.

"Oh, you're going to be fun, your majesty."

"Am...am I?"

"Yes, very much so."

He moved between her legs and this part she knew. This part she understood. She put her legs around him and lifted her hips, bracing herself for the expected stab of pain. It hurt every time the king entered her, and it never occurred to her that it would be any different with John. It seemed like it was more her problem than his, and yet, when he slid into her, it didn't even sting. She knew he was bigger than his father, though, because her walls stretched around him more than she ever stretched around the king. Plus, she never, ever felt so full. And yet, there was still no pain, no discomfort. Nothing but an amazing pressure, a choking pleasure that made her throat tight.

"Do you like that?"

She quickly nodded. He pulled back and thrust forward. "Tell me."

"I like it."

"Do you love it?"

"Yes...please don't stop, John. Please.

This feels so good."

The king would rut above her for a handful of minutes, panting and grunting and sweating, and she would do her best not to look him in the eyes. But she couldn't stop staring at the prince, couldn't get her fill of him. His face changed, reflecting the pleasure she felt with every motion of his hips. His muscles rippled under his skin, drawing her attention and her touch, and then her mouth. She kissed his throat and chest, her lips fluttering over every bit of him that she could reach. Her hands went to his hips, palms pressed against his chiseled lines, drawing him back inside of her each time he pulled out.

They had no trouble moving together, their young, tight bodies finding a mutually satisfying rhythm. His attention returned to her nipples, and even though she thought she knew what to expect, the new wave of sensation took her by complete surprise. It was even more intense than before with his shaft moving inside, and she automatically clenched down every time he bit or pinched her. She felt more sensitive than ever before, and a whisper of contact was enough to light her fire from the inside out. She felt herself being carried away, picked up by the waves to be brought to a place she didn't know, a place she couldn't begin to understand. She'd hoped that bringing John to her bed would be productive, but she never, ever assumed it would elevate her so far above what she accepted as her life.

"I should stop..."

"What?" She wrapped her legs around him, refusing to let him move, his length fully sheathed. "No."

"I'm close, sweetheart."

She shook her head. "Don't stop."

"But..."

"Don't. Stop." She pushed her hips up, slid down, and then did it again. He moaned, tried to resist, but there was nothing he could do to escape the heat, the tight friction, or her unrelenting need. His body knew what to do, knew that this wasn't difficult or complicated. He took her by the hips and the quality of his strokes changed, became shorter and faster. His teeth scraped across her nipples on a hard, downward stroke, and the world went dark around her. She turned her head into his arm, biting down as hard as she could as everything inside shattered. Her instincts took over, driving her hips until another flare of pleasure ignited. Her eyes squeezed shut, the world tilting beneath her in the dark. He was the only thing stable, the only thing she could cling to as the bliss buffeted her body. He suddenly froze, his member jerking against her flesh as he emptied himself into her waiting and fertile body. Sealing the pact between them for the rest of their lives.

10 COUPLETS WITHOUT RHYME

Sam found himself searching for William's face everywhere he traveled, even when he knew for a fact that his friend was hundreds of miles away. He couldn't help it, having fallen into that habit in the past year. Every time he left his little cottage, he had only one goal in mind—one real purpose. Even if he stepped out on some business that was ostensibly non-William-related, he ended up walking towards the other man's cottage. He was homesick now, and the nostalgic yearning made him all the more eager to see William—or some visual approximation of his beloved face. Sam was growing desperate and he was willing to take whatever he could get.

Growing? No. That was wrong. He'd

crossed that line months earlier. Maybe even the night he formally met the brilliant man who would become his closest friend. Their entire relationship was marked with an edge of desperation because Sam could never be close enough, could never learn enough, and could never share enough with him. Their greatest intimacy still fell well short of his greatest hopes, even though he could honestly say that he was closer to William than he was to anybody else, including his own wife. Gradually, he came to realize that his dissatisfaction would never leave—not unless he did. So he hunted around for the opportunity to leave and found it with a friend who was willing to give him an allowance to travel abroad to Germany to continue his studies. It was a gift from heaven when he needed it the most, but that didn't stop him from crying pathetically the night before he boarded the steamer—and every night after that for a week.

But fleeing to the continent did nothing to ease the pain in his chest. Even wine tinged with opium did little to help him sleep these days. Writing was a mess; he had no end of inspiration but for once, the words he wanted were too far out of reach. He had no shortage of other words. They positively spewed from him, like pus escaping from an infection, but he hated them for being putrid. Hackneyed. If he had nothing new to say, he shouldn't be writing at all. But that was the danger of leaving Will. When they were together, Sam's entire being was filled with lights and the words came to him from the mouths of a heavenly chorus. Or maybe they leapt directly from Will's heart to his own pen. Without William there, what could he ever hope to write? He was wasting his allowance, accomplishing none of the work he'd been sent to do it. Translation was all he seemed capable of, except he had it all backwards. Instead of taking poetry from German to English, he merely rewrote Will's verse in German.

They were still in semi-regular correspondence, but there was coldness between the lines of his graceful script. Sam restrained himself in his responses, though he found himself wadding leaf after leaf into an angry mass, tossing them aside and starting all over again. He couldn't say too much. Leaving was supposed to make it easier, but his heart still ached like a raw nerve, the pain driving him deeper and deeper into his bottles, deeper and deeper into his despair. But at the same time, the letters, both received and sent, were his greatest solace. Sometimes he craved the comfort of Will's company so greatly that writing a letter to him and re-reading the few he'd received were almost as good as touching the back of his hand and listening to his laugh.

No, that was a lie he tried to tell himself. The truth was that nothing could be as good as being with William. And no amount of separation would heal this wound, the festering gash in his heart. It wasn't the first time he became too attached to another man, and he promised to himself he would never make that mistake again. It could only end horribly, and he was sensitive to every slight, every little hurt and twinge.

Did William miss him at all? Did he think about Sam when he was waking? Or before he drifted to sleep? Did he spare any thoughts at all to Sam and could he ever find out?

His temporary home in Germany was comfortable by anybody's standards, but he too often felt shut-in and trapped by the cozy walls. He fled to the surrounding countryside at every possible chance, planning long, elaborate walks that took him across half the country and left him feeling alive yet too tired to dwell over much on Will. He should be thinking important thoughts and composing masterpieces, but what was once such a productive time was now largely devoted to the nuances of the smile he missed so much.

On the fourth evening of one such walk,

he came across an inn beside the road. He may have walked right past it, but the smell of the pie cooling on the window enticed him through the door. The heavenly aroma was more pronounced inside the small building, and his stomach grumbled, insisting he tarry there and enjoy what promised to be an amazing meal. They happened to have a spare bed and Sam happened to have enough coins to reserve it and a plate of the wife's delicious food. He turned to survey the tables, absently searching for the face he knew he'd never see.

Except there he was. Sam took an involuntary step forward, his eyes wide, certain he was seeing things. That couldn't be Will sitting in the corner, even though he was wearing Will's old, ratty coat; even though he had Will's profile and his hawkish nose; and even though he was writing in Will's blue journal with his studios frown.

"William?"

He looked up and smiled, and Sam thought he must be dreaming. "Sam? Imagine the good luck in finding you here!"

"What are you doing here?"

"I'm traveling to Munich. I thought I would surprise you with a visit. Are you surprised?"

"Yes. Yes, most pleasantly so."

"Sit down then and let's break bread. I have messages for you and some pamphlets I thought you would enjoy."

Grinning, feeling like he'd just doped up again, he took his seat at William's side and prepared to bask in his presence for the rest of the night.

They drank copious amounts of wine, far more than they ever drank together back home. But there nobody knew who they were, and they both took advantage of that fact. In England, Sam had a wife and William had a sister that demanded his attention. There was no sense of freedom, even when they fled to the surrounding countryside and walked for hours through the hills. But this inn was different, and so they drank and they laughed and they talked, unconsciously laying themselves bare. Neither wanted the night to end, and when it was time to retire, William followed Sam to his room with a new bottle of wine and a plate of bread from the kitchen.

The room was small, but when William stepped inside and closed the door, it became absolutely tiny. Sam turned around and William was right in his face, standing toe to toe with him, bottle in hand. The room had a bed and a chair with a desk, and there wasn't any room to maneuver. A cloud of booze hung between them, and there was enough light from the lamp in the room to let Sam see the green flecks buried in William's brown eyes. His eyes reminded Sam of the newness of spring. His smile was summer. No, not just his smile. His whole mouth. He would taste of summer, too.

Nobody knew them there. Maybe if he found out, if he tested this hypothesis, nobody would ever have to know? The act wouldn't have to leave the confines of that room, and if Will hated him for it, maybe that would make it easier. Because sooner or later, he would have to walk away from William and he would have to stay gone.

Unless William kissed him back?

Especially if William kissed him back.

He didn't give himself a chance to change his mind. All of his thoughts flashed through his mind in a second and then he was moving, tilting his head and tentatively touching their mouths together. It wasn't really a proper kiss. All he did was rest there for a moment and then straighten again, hoping to do nothing more than announce his intentions. He studied Will's face, expecting to see shock and anger, but there was no surprise in his eyes, and he didn't seem particularly angry either.

"I had certain...dreams," Will said softly.

"I wasn't sure if you shared in the same sort of dreams, but I thought, perhaps, Germany would be a good place to find out."

"Dreams," Sam echoed. He was comfortable with the language of dreams, the exaggerated imagery of the long-repressed desires of the soul. Opium helped him talk in the language of dreams, and perhaps that was why he could never shake himself from that seductive hold. He moved into another kiss, William meeting halfway, and this time it was more than a request. He licked the tip of his tongue over Will's bottom lip, teasing himself with the faint taste of wine. William opened his mouth, allowing him to enter and flood his mouth with the sweet taste of wine and flowers, and yes, there was definitely the heat of summer there. A dark feeling of delight surged within him, reminding him of his most intense opium experiences. It wasn't just the pleasure of William's mouth but the knowledge that he shouldn't be doing this. He never ever gave in to the temptation even though William was not the first temptation he encountered.

The combination of the wine and the kiss made him lightheaded, and when their mouths pulled apart, he gasped and stumbled back. William went with him, his hands on Sam's shoulders, holding him steady as he sat down on the edge of the hard mattress. There was really only enough room for one person on the narrow frame, but Sam didn't think twice before pulling William down with him. They lay on their sides, facing each other, their groins touching, their mouths nearly touching. William propped himself up on his elbow and reached out with his other hand. He briefly touched Sam's shoulder and his chest—as if he was looking for the perfect place to let his palm rest. He found the perfect spot on the back of Sam's neck, and he pulled him into a slow, deliberate kiss.

Nobody had ever kissed Sam like that before. Not that he had received many kisses before that moment. His wife's kisses were short and perfunctory, and he'd only ever scraped up the courage to kiss one other girl, but she wouldn't have him and didn't want to marry him. William kissed him as if he'd been waiting for the chance for a very long time. The force of that kiss answered all the questions he had before—of course Will thought about him, and missed him, and maybe he shared Sam's yearning. There was no "maybe" about it. No, judging from the force of the kiss, the raw sensuality of his mouth moving over Sam's, they were on the same page once again. They'd always had a certain understanding between them, a magic chemistry that Sam never shared with anybody else. They were kindred spirits—uniquely matched souls—and that was a fact Sam knew since he first read Will's poetry, four years before they ever met.

This was supposed to be unnatural, and their attraction was supposed to be wrong—wrong enough to send them to hell. But Sam knew hell. He'd been through the depths of suffering without William, and he could do it again but only if he could have the memories of this night. They tugged at each other's clothes, though the most they could do was to make the occasional holes and opening, revealing patches of skin to hungry fingers. He felt a shock every time skin touched skin—an eruption of pleasure and a spark of fire under his skin. Each spark sizzled to his groin, and he wished he could explain it—wished he could understand. Maybe that was the purpose of poetry, but if that were true, they were all cowards because nobody even got close to addressing the situation. Even the most passionate love poetry couldn't lend the necessary vocabulary to process or understand the increasingly intense sensations.

William shifted their positions, rolling Sam onto his back and settling his weight over him, hip to hip. He shifted his hips, grinding his hard erection into Sam's, the painful restriction of his trousers being not enough to distract him from the satisfaction of William's weight and the intense pleasure against his throbbing flesh. He shifted again and Sam rose up to meet him, their hips coming together hard enough to make them both groan. They quickly fell into rhythm, rocking against each other while their mouths fused together, their tongues engaging in a familiar slow dance that left Sam shaking like a leaf in the autumn wind. Not just wind. An entire thunderstorm was brewing inside of him, shaking his very foundations.

He opened his eyes to study William's face and saw a reflection of the lightning crashing inside of him. It was there, in his spring-colored eyes. He reached between their bodies with new intention, and this time he was successful in unbuttoning and unlacing William's trousers. Seconds later, he enjoyed success with his own trousers, and their erections sprang from the tight garments, sliding against each other as if eager to make each other's acquaintances.

"I'm going to show you something."

"What?" Sam asked.

"As I said, I'm going to show you something. Not tell you something." With that, he pushed his weight up and stood. Sam nearly panicked, but William shoved his pants down and then resumed his place on top of Sam, only he was sitting with his back to him. "It's a little trick I learned at public school."

It never occurred to Sam that this wasn't Will's first indiscretion. He'd denied himself for so long that he assumed everybody else did the same. At the same time, he was more than relieved to know that Will had some idea of what to do because he honestly had none at all. He wanted to be close to Will, but his mind continuously shied away from the most likely scenarios until he was left with nothing more than a vague, but intense, desire; a desire finally put into physical reality when William angled Sam's hard length and closed his mouth around him, swallowing most of him down the moist corridor of his throat.

Sam was an intuitive guy, and he knew what he needed to do once he could swim through the thick fog and make sense of what was happening. He gripped William by the hips and pulled him back, pulling his thick cock between his legs and angling it downward. He'd never done this before, but he could follow William's lead, and he wanted to do anything to make

William feel good. Amazing. As amazing as he felt at that moment, with the liquid heat of his mouth closing around him again and again.

As soon as his lips went around the velvety crown, William pushed down. Sam gagged, jerking with surprise, and tried to yank away, but there wasn't room to move his head, trapped as he was between William's thighs. William shifted his hips again, pushing down until Sam was gagging. This time, Sam didn't try to pull away. He inhaled through his nose and forced himself to concentrate and relax his throat so on the third thrust, William could sheath himself in the column. Once Will filled the passage, he swallowed, squeezing around the shaft, moaning as Will returned the favor.

Desperate, lust-stricken, and unable to hold themselves back, they humped their hips in sporadic but rapid tempo. Neither of them moved gracefully but they both moved sincerely, with genuine need fueling every thrust of their hips. Sam dug his fingers into William's ass, getting to the point where he literally was dragging William down into his mouth.

Sam felt like he was running through the hills—felt like he was flying above the rolling green and throwing himself headlong into the furious winds and glorious lightning. He surrendered entirely to that sense of freedom, and the wind lifted him and carried him forward until he realized he was about to soar right over an edge he never even noticed before. It reminded him of poetry, of the loose lines and unrolling words that could go on and on, stretching to infinity until somebody smoothed the rough edges and pushed the words onto the page.

The orgasm swept through him, pristine and shuddering pleasure that broke over him and left him shaking, weak, and exhausted until his cock was finally spent. That's when Will shuddered his way to his own climax, his thick, salty fluid flowing straight down the back of his throat. He swallowed automatically, taking down every drop until William sat up, pulling himself free. He turned around and settled down again, wedging himself between Sam and the wall. He could have gone to his own room and could have left Sam alone and trembling, but he settled in close, his head resting on Sam's chest.

The next morning, Sam woke up alone, an empty bottle of wine on the floor and a half-empty bottle of opium beside it. No sign of William anywhere. Sam looked around the room and collapsed back against the mattress. If he didn't get up, he could tell himself William was outside enjoying an early morning stroll before breakfast. Yes, that was what he wanted to do. He closed his eyes again and imagined the comfort of William's arms around him once again.

11 THE NOVICE SEDUCTION

Katarina was Allgott's dark-eyed daughter, the youngest of two and always a little bitter because she lacked her sister's fair beauty. Even so, she was the apple of her father's eye, and when it was her turn to live at his home rather than the convent, she was given free rein and more or less allowed to rule the household. But she was a smart girl, and she knew her days of relative freedom were coming to an end. Their father only had the resources to marry off one of his daughters, and Katarina knew it wouldn't be her. She would be sent off to the convent permanently, a prisoner held there forever with no hope of escape or having her own family. The only way to ensure that wouldn't happen to her was to find a man before Cecilia did. And if she couldn't find one to marry, she could at least find one to enjoy.

When Arn Folkesson rode with his men into their small village, Katarina was fetching water from the well. She paused in her work, unable to do anything but watch him until he disappeared around the corner and out of sight. He was near her age, and easily the most handsome man Katarina had ever seen in her life. She'd never seen him before, but she knew exactly who he was. Not only were they expecting him, but his reputation had spread far and wide, and everybody knew that Folke's son was back from the monastery, prepared to defend his father's lands against the tyranny of the pretender on the throne. She lifted the pail, sloshing water over the sides as she hurried to meet the men at her father's house, giddy with excitement.

They feasted well that night, killing two goats for the supper, and the mead flowed freely. Arn drank until his cheeks flushed and his eyes twinkled, and he seemed completely overwhelmed by the men around him. Watching him eat, it was easy to forget all the stories about him. He didn't seem like any warrior she ever met. His horse was taller than all the others, and so when he sat astride it, he seemed taller. But at the table, he was shorter than most of the men, and while they all wore their battle scars on their faces and arms, Arn wasn't scarred at all. Katarina was fascinated by him, and she made sure that he had her full attention all night— and that he knew it. Every time he looked at her, his cheeks seemed to redder, his eyes seemed to be brighter. Had he ever been with a woman? Katarina didn't think so. He had been raised by monks, after all. He probably thought it was a sin. She refilled his cup often, personally seeing to it that he always had enough.

The feast only ended when everybody passed out. As her father started to sway, she led him away to his room and ordered her thane to see to Arn. Within minutes, the entire hall was silent except for the drunken snoring of the men, which rumbled off the ceiling and walls like thunder. Once she made sure her father was well, she slipped through to where Arn was staying the night. As the guest of honor, he had his own room as well. A single candle burned in the corner, flickering as she opened the door and let herself into the room. He was sitting on the edge of his bed, looking up with bleary eyes as she approached.

"Katarina..."

"Are you well, my lord?"

"I'm afraid I've had too much mead."

"Do you have a headache? I can help

you with that."

"Should you be here?" He asked thickly.

"Shh. Don't worry about that." She pulled at the laces at the front of her dress, but he reached up, staying her hand.

"Don't."

"Why not? Have you ever looked on a woman?"

"No. It's a sin."

"A sin?" She shook her head. "They only tell you that because they're old and jealous."

He jumped to his feet, but immediately swayed, and she took him by the arm and guided him back down to the bed.

"Don't be so hasty," she admonished.

"Lying with a woman outside of marriage is a sin," he said, more forcefully. "I will not commit the sin of adultery."

She heard him but she didn't care. She knew how men worked, and that often, their mouths and their bodies were at war with each other. Just because he said one thing didn't mean he truly meant it. It didn't even mean he'd remember it in five minutes when he discovered just how much fun this particular sin was.

"Nobody will ever have to know," she promised him, pulling at his tunic. He tried to resist her, but she was quick and adept and quickly had his tunic tossed aside. His body was solid, his muscles thick from years of hard physical labor at the monastery. Somehow, his simple clothes shielded his perfection, but she realized how wrong her earlier assessment was. There was nothing boyish about this man, even though he was unlike any other man she'd ever known. She caressed his shoulder and stroked her fingers over his chest, petting him like she'd pet a skittish horse. His full pink lips parted with a slight gasp as she touched him, and she knew that nobody else ever caressed him like this. He was untouched and pure, unaware of the pleasure he could so easily possess.

He wouldn't be ignorant any more after that night. Katarina was going to personally see to that. She cupped his cheek and drew his mouth towards hers. He tasted of roasted meat and mead, and she parted her lips, allowing him to dip his tongue into her mouth. He made another small sound of surprise, and she pressed herself closer, molding herself against him from breast to hip. Without breaking the kiss, she took his hand and guided it to her right breast, holding it over the soft mound until his fingers closed, squeezing her gently. She smiled in encouragement, knowing he'd feel it even if he couldn't see it, and arched her back into his touch.

"You're so soft," he murmured.

"You have no idea," she promised. She

hiked her dress up past her hips and guided his hand down her torso, past her stomach. He resisted though, his arm suddenly becoming a branch of oak that she couldn't budge. "What's wrong?"

"I told you. This is wrong. When I left the monastery, I vowed I would not become worldly. I've never sinned like this. I'm not going to start now."

"You've never sinned? Is murder not a sin?"

He looked momentarily stricken. "I...that was...I have already sought forgiveness for that boy's death."

"Then seek forgiveness for this, too." She reached between his legs, fingers closing around his excitement. He was as hard as anybody she'd ever been with, and there was no way for him to deny that. He couldn't ignore it, either. Not while she stroked him. She shoved his clothing out of the way, fishing his thick tool from the inconvenient material. He may have been able to protest before, but now with her hot hand wrapped around his shaft, he was silent. She kissed him again, her hand slowly traveling up and down, each pump of her wrist a promise of pleasures he couldn't even comprehend.

Arn wanted to push her away from him

and leave the room. He wanted to call upon God for help and strength. He wanted to catch his breath and try to clear his thoughts. He'd never felt so muddled before, never had to travel through so much fog. In the monastery, everything made perfect sense. He knew God's law and God's will, and all he had to do was serve Him in all His glory. There were no choices to make, no decisions that belonged to him, and no temptation to overcome. But now, there was nothing but confusion and unease. He didn't feel God's spirit anywhere around him. He'd never felt more alone in his life.

Except, he wasn't alone. Katarina was gently coaxing him with her mouth and her hand, waking things in him that he never even knew existed. He didn't think the sensations were coming from him at all. What if she was a witch? What if she was conducting some sort of magic to cloud his brain and turn him into a servant of the devil? He didn't want to be a slave to Lucifer, but neither did he want to do what was necessary to put an end to this encounter. He was stronger than she was, and faster. He could shove her away and flee. He could start shouting, accusing her of witchcraft, waking the whole hall to come to his rescue. True, she was the daughter of his host, but witchcraft was witchcraft. She shouldn't be allowed to get away with it just because she chose to practice in her father's house.

But he couldn't do it. It almost felt like he was physically incapable. When he opened his mouth, she only kissed him and all the sound he could muster was a moan. When he put a hand up to push her away, he only ended up cupping her breast and then sliding his fingers through her hair. When he tried to pray for strength, she tightened her grip and pumped her wrist faster, replacing the desire to pray with a desire that was much more powerful. Primal and frightening. Something he shouldn't be exposed to at all. Something that was too dangerous for him. But it seemed to be the exact thing she wanted.

"I don't know what to do," he finally admitted.

"I know. But don't worry. It's so easy."

She lay back on the bed and pulled him down. He had to follow her lead, and it was like when Brother Guilbert taught him how to fight. At first, his body didn't know what to do and everything about the situation was wrong and awkward. He knew nothing about holding a sword when Guilbert gave him his first lessons, but now nobody could best him. He dragged his hand down her body and between her legs, wondering exactly what she was pulling him towards. He sucked his breath in sharply, stunned by how soft she was. His mind raced through memories and comparisons, but not even the downy wool on a baby lamb could compare to the softness of her nest of hair, or the slick, exquisite feel of her flesh.

"It feels good, doesn't it?" She asked gently.

"It'll feel even better if you use your staff." She opened her legs wider and lifted up, moving against his hand. He slid his fingers up and down her slit, then found her opening and he couldn't even breathe as he pushed forward, sinking his finger all the way to the knuckle. Her walls fluttered around him, and she moaned and began to move, grinding against him. His staff jerked violently, and the pain in his groin was intense enough to stop his breathing. His lungs burned and his head swam, and somewhere under the buzzing in his ears, he heard her plea for more.

She was right. It was easy. Once he lined himself up with her, all he had to do was follow the heat. As soon as he entered her, all of his other thoughts and fears disappeared. There was no fear of sinning because he forgot all about God and the training he'd received since he was a small child. She washed all of that away when she closed around him.

"Just take it slow," she whispered in his ear.

The candle wasn't close enough to light her face, and when he closed her eyes, it was like he was with a dark phantom. He did as he was told, too well trained to ignore the direct order of a more learned person. He rocked slowly, pushing himself to greater heights of pleasure with every slow stroke. She touched him everywhere, her hands moving over his back and shoulders, then down his chest. He liked the way she touched him. He knew things could hurt. He'd lived through a lifetime of endless pain in one form or another. It was an accepted part of his existence. What else was there? What more could there be?

But now he knew. There was this pleasure. There was this abandon. There was letting go of everything in the quest for something...divine.

It was fun, too. He loved physical exertion, but there was no exercise or fight that could compare to this exhilaration. He didn't disrupt the pace, but he wanted to go faster and harder. He wanted to push himself as he would in a battle, take himself to the very extremes of his physical limits. He worried about hurting her though, didn't want to push her too far because she was so much smaller than he was. Fragile even. He did his best to keep his weight off her, tried to avoid crushing her even though she kept pulling him closer, kept trying to eliminate any space between them.

She wasn't completely silent and he wasn't either. If anybody in the hall emerged from their mead-soaked dreams, they would definitely know exactly what was going on, even if they couldn't name who the two lovers were. "That's it...so good...oh you're so good at this..." she whispered and he grunted in return, his chest rumbling at every stroke.

He stopped quite suddenly, his chest heaving and his frame shaking. Something changed. He felt as though he was on a precipice, his entire body aching and tingling at once. It was the rush of a good battle and the transcendent beauty of a choir of voices praising God in heaven.

"Don't stop," she murmured, rocking her hips. He tried to resist at first, his former doubts temporarily gaining a foothold while he tried to bring his racing heart and jittery thoughts under control. But she rocked her hips again, used her body to make his move again. His hips acted as if they were completely independent from the rest of him. He had no sense of control as he began to move.

"Faster," she urged. "You can go faster. As fast as you want. Like you're riding the wind."

She bucked her hips with each word, and he found himself following her lead again, moving faster and faster until he thought sparks would fly up from the friction they created. He slammed into her smaller frame, and far from hurting her, she seemed to enjoy it. She dropped her head back, her profile catching the dim light of the candle, and he saw her eyes were closed and her lips were open. All of the bliss washing through him was reflected on her face, and seeing it so clearly had an immediate effect on him. He rushed back to the precipice that stopped him before, and then he flung himself into the unknown, falling into the deepest well of pleasure as everything pulled tight and he emptied himself inside her.

"Oh yes," she keened, her body shaking as she fell over her own precipice. He held her as she trembled, her walls convulsing around him, milking him for everything he had. "Oh Arn. That was so good. You did such a good job."

He absorbed the praise, but he was already thinking about the inevitable punishment. Nothing escaped God's notice, after all.

12 THE PROLOGUE OF PLEASURE

Young women traveled from as far away as Athens and even Persia to study under the tutelage of Sappho. Some were sent by their parents, but others ran away from their homes and families, sacrificing everything to have the chance to learn from the great woman herself. Anactoria was one who had to flee her family, including the man she was betrothed to, but she did so without fear. In Athens, everybody talked about Sappho and her poetry was widely recited. Anactoria never spent a day without listening to the beautiful lyrics, and when she learned of a party that was traveling from Athens to Lesbos, she bribed passage for herself and snuck out of the city under the cover of darkness.

Sappho was nothing like she thought she'd be and yet everything Anactoria imagined she must be. She was short – shorter even than Anactoria – with dark eyes and hair so black it seemed to be violet. At first, Anactoria was convinced her eyes were a deep shade of brown, but upon closer inspection she saw no difference between the iris and the pupil. They formed one continuous black circle, twin obsidian pools that Anactoria couldn't look away from. Her voice had a musical quality, like a lyre played with light fingers, and everything she said sounded like a poem, even when she was dealing with mundane daily business. Her laugh didn't just have a musical quality, it was music. Beautiful and simple like a bird's song, uplifting and unexpected. Her features were fine, and her skin warmed and toasted by the sun, which she never tried to avoid. She could usually be found outside, her hair falling in dark waves down her bare shoulders as she stared out over the water. That's how she worked, and even when she didn't have ink and papyrus in front of her, she was writing.

Anactoria hoped Sappho would look upon her favorably, maybe even spare a word to her, but she never expected to catch the poet's attention. She did have a reputation for beauty in Athens, and her father had a fair pick of men who were eager to marry her. Her hair fell down to her waist, as straight as straw and the same golden color. She'd been kept indoors and protected from the sun by her anxious mother, and so she was a good bit more fair than Sappho and most of the other girls at the Academy. A small, sharp nose and a pointed chin framed her Cupid's bow mouth, high cheekbones balancing her features and giving her a rather striking look. She didn't remember smiling at all in her former life, but once she reached Lesbos, she couldn't keep the smile from her face. Maybe her ceaseless smile was what ultimately attracted Sappho's attention to her. The poet said more than once that she loved beautiful things, and her love seemed to be as endless as the blue sea surrounding them.

Anactoria continued through her days as the model student, ignorant of the additional attention she was receiving from her head mistress. She continued on in her ignorance right up until Sappho summoned her to her room. As far as she knew, Sappho didn't meet with her students in her own private quarters, but it still never occurred to her that her affections might be returned. Sappho rose as she entered the room and glided across the room with her quiet steps, a cool breeze blowing off the ocean and through the open door, dancing through her hair and making her robe rustle around her legs. She stopped within touching distance, reaching up to untie the belt cinching her robes together. Anactoria could only stare as the material fell away, revealing her proud breasts and rounded hips. Hair as dark and soft as that on her head jutted from the twin column of her thighs, and she was golden brown everywhere. Her perfume wafted on the breeze, blowing around Anactoria, creating an intoxicating cloud. Her mouth ran dry and she thought she should say something, or do something, but she was at a loss.

"Anactoria?" Her name rolled off Sappho's tongue, the warm, thick sound flowing down her spine and pooling between her legs. "May I place a kiss on your soft lips?"

The question felt like a kiss. She nodded, and Sappho stepped forward, taking her by the arms. She pulled their bodies together, and Anactoria could feel the heat of her skin through her robes. Suddenly, the soft, rich fabric felt like the roughest, poorest muslin, like sacks made for grain. It was her skin, suddenly sensitive to everything and flushed from the blood roaring through her veins. She had never felt so warm, but she was shivering too, goose bumps dancing down her back. Sappho tilted her chin up, kissed first her left cheek, her right, and then the corner of her mouth. Her lips were softer than flower petals, and so hot they burned right through her flesh right to her soul. When she finally found Anactoria's lips, the caress felt like the fulfillment of a promise made long ago.

Anactoria sighed and parted her lips, allowing Sappho full entry. She felt a brief tug and then her robe loosened. The garment fell away with a whisper, and the relief of Sappho's skin was immediate. She could feel her softness everywhere, and that still wasn't enough. She pressed herself even closer to her teacher, her body awakening to the possibility of true pleasure for the first time in her young life. At first, the kiss seemed awkward to her, but Sappho was her teacher in all things, and soon she learned what she needed to know. The feeling between them shifted as Anactoria's shocked shyness gave way to a new understanding and the confidence that accompanied that. She could feel Sappho smile in the kiss, feel her approval and pleasure with each movement of her lips and flicker of her tongue.

Sappho pulled away from the kiss and took Anactoria's hand, leading her away from the discarded clothes. She followed Sappho into the next room that held the bed. Anactoria's eyes widened at the sheer number of phalluses present on display. Did Sappho always keep them out like that or was this in preparation of Anactoria's visit? She sent a questioning look to her teacher, but there were no answers or explanations. She gently pushed Anactoria down to the bed, their mouths joining together again before they hit the soft mattress.

She couldn't get enough of Sappho's kisses, chasing her mouth when she eased back, wrapping her arms around the smaller frame, her entire body yearning for something. Anactoria didn't know quite what, but she was eager to learn. Sappho managed to break away from her hungry lips, though she didn't go far, kissing a trail down her throat. Anactoria arched her head back, instantly shocked by the powerful sensations inspired by the brief contact. She'd touched her neck countless times, but it was like she never experienced a second of contact before Sappho turned her attentions on her body. She rained kisses down on her throat and her shoulders, each one equally soft, equally hot. She moved slowly, kissing over the swells of her breasts, smoothing her lips over each globe. Anactoria already felt like she was drowning, but she didn't need to gasp for breath until Sappho pulled her nipple between her lips and applied the briefest pressure, sucking ever so lightly. It was still intense enough to send a very pleasant sensation to the area between her legs. It was funny, she rarely gave that triangle any thought at all, but now it was demanding her attention – no, demanding Sappho's attention. When it became too urgent to ignore for another second, she took Sappho's small hand in hers and guided it down her body.

Sappho smiled again as her knuckles brushed over the damp curls. Her fingertips traveled up and down, seemed to be touching her everywhere and nowhere all at once. She whimpered, her legs unconsciously spreading while her hips rocked. At first, she thought simply feeling Sappho's touch between her legs would be enough to ease the growing ache there, but that couldn't be further from the truth. It did nothing to ease things, only sharpened the need she felt. She whimpered again as her fingers slid between her labia, and the first touch against her swollen clitoris was powerful enough to pull a shout from her throat.

"Oh, what did you...what was that?"

"It was pleasure, my little Anactoria. Would you like more?"

"Yes," she whispered, desperate for more.

"Good girl." She rubbed her finger in a steady circle, grinding down on the throbbing flesh, making her buck and jerk beneath Sappho's light body. The sensation filled her world completely and for long minutes, she didn't know anything except the rising and falling pleasure, like gentle waves rolling over the coast. But like the ocean, the waves pulled back eventually, not disappearing but not quite enough either. The ache returned in full force, gripping her completely, throbbing through every inch of her from her knees to her throat. Her eyes flew open and she was surprised to see Sappho's face just a few inches above hers, her dark eyes noting and reading every emotion that marched across her face.

"Are you ready for more?"

Anactoria nodded eagerly. Whatever more there was, she wanted it. There had to be something to ease this pain, to satisfy the hunger that threatened to consume her entirely. Sappho pulled away completely, much to her disappointment, leaving her shivering and cold without the perfect, reassuring heat of her body. She pushed herself up on her elbows, watching as Sappho glided around the room, until she came to a stop in front of a thin phallus carved from pink marble and polished until it gleamed. Anactoria didn't have any first-hand knowledge, but she'd seen other phalluses, and this one seemed particularly lifelike, complete with a ridge at the crown and what looked like a vein bulging along the bottom.

"Have you ever been penetrated?"

Anactoria shook her head.

"You don't have anything to fear, my darling. You're more than prepared for this, but I'll go slowly. Now lay back and relax."

Anactoria did as she was told, eyes fluttering shut while she took slow, steadying breaths. She didn't need the warning or the reassurances – she was ready. She was more than ready. It felt like she'd been waiting for this her whole life – at the very least, since the first moment she felt Sappho's lips on her own. With her knees out and her heels touching, she waited for the cool touch of the marble against her overheated skin. It wasn't cool when it touched her, though, and she realized that Sappho must have had oil warming precisely for this purpose. It smelled pleasant, too, like it had been infused with roses and honeysuckle.

"Deep breath in," Sappho murmured against Anactoria's mouth, their lips barely touching. Anactoria inhaled, and she felt the nudge of the hard phallus at her opening. She exhaled and took another deep breath and Sappho chose that moment to thrust the phallus forward, pushing past her maiden barrier, filling her with as much as she could take.

Anactoria expected there to be some pain, but there was none. It was the least painful moment of her life, when all the good that was possible came to fruition and expanded beneath her skin. She rose off the bed on the force of her pleasure, and Sappho slid an arm beneath her, holding her close as her tongue invaded her mouth. Anactoria hooked her leg over Sappho's hip, their bodies entwining as closely as they could while the shaft slowly slid in and out of her gripping channel.

"Don't try to hold yourself back, darling. Just give in to what you're feeling. Let it wash over you...let it become everything. You're only a single drop in an infinite ocean. Surrender to that." Her low words were hypnotic, as intense and captivating as her touch. Her hand never stopped moving, and she felt like she was literally being pumped full of light. She did as her instructor told her, surrendering entirely and not clinging to any conscious thought. There was no reality beyond the safe cocoon of Sappho's arms. The pleasure grew with every stroke, constantly urging her to heights she never felt before, never conceived of.

Sudden pressure settled on her nub, and the light flared inside of her. The sound she made was unlike anything she'd ever heard, certainly unlike anything she'd ever produced. Everybody at the academy must have heard her, as the shout traveled to the very top of the spheres. She knew because that's where she was, far above everything else. And when she floated back down, Sappho was cradling her closely.

"Now we can get started," she said sweetly.

"Started?"

"This is merely the prologue for you," Sappho promised.

AUTHOR'S NOTE

Readers: I want to expand a few of the stories to see where the characters can be explored further. If there are any of the stories that you would like to read more about again, I'd love to hear from you!

Visit my blog at http://www.kelliegranier.com

Join my newsletter for free exclusive previews
http://www.kelliegranier.com/in

Follow me on Twitter at
http://www.twitter.com/kelliegranier

Like my page on Facebook at
http://www.facebook.com/kelliegranier

Discover my books at major ebook retailers everywhere.